FORUM

JOSH WARDRIP

TAILWINDS PRESS

Tailwinds Press
P.O. Box 2283, Radio City Station
New York, NY 10101-2283
www.tailwindspress.com

Published in the United States of America
ISBN: 978-1-7356016-6-3
1st ed. 2022

FORUM

for Nikki and Olivia

Do not be deceived,
    O my friend, by shameful gains,
    for the posthumous acclaim of fame
alone reveals the life of men who are dead and gone
to both chroniclers and poets. The kindly
    excellence of Croesus does not perish,
but universal execration overwhelms Phalaris, that man
of pitiless spirit who burned men in his bronze bull,
and no lyres in banquet halls welcome him
in gentle fellowship with boys' voices.

                                        - Pindar, *Pythian* 1

MATERIAL SUPPORT

Two nothing days in the hotel room When I couldn't
stand it anymore I took a walk to the convenience mart
People slouched around the lot and black squad cars
parted the air skimming back and forth and in and out
ubiquitous and sick with boredom always that way never
some other way He said something the guy lingering by
the entrance as I opened the door I let this stuff go usually
but I was blasted and because I was that way and maybe
something more I replied in kind A store employee rushed
out and yelled at the person chased him off Did they put
it in their job postings required skills must be able to lift
thirty pounds must be able to manage aggressive vagrants
Inside a respite from the sweat and malaise like a *portal* in
a banal fantasy quiet and cool chilly almost Hypervigilant
the three store workers ruled from behind the counter I
wondered what mighty weapons trove lay concealed
underneath what guarantor of commerce unimpeded I
searched the aisles got what I needed checked out The
cashier handed me the change gave a solemn nod On the
way out too rushed or anxious or partitioned off from
things by a wall of fog I knocked the door right into a guy

trying to come in He was young angry built A tenuous second or two but then okay apology accepted and he went inside Out in the lot and this always happens they asked for money sorry no I said so they switched tactics and asked for a beer instead I took the plastic bag out of my satchel opened it and showed its contents Nine-volt batteries rolls of black electrical tape a box of razor blades A blade might be your best bet And they growled a little fuck you and they walked away

FORUM OF THE OX

Because it would be stupid I won't say I intuited what would happen later but Zlnka had seemed different even if it was hard to discern because what is there to discern when all is flat but to ask if he was okay would've violated our agreement which was hardly an agreement at all but a tacit understanding between us It was the silliest thing you could ask are you okay because I'm here I'm not okay Yet his absence at breakfast and skewed manner suggested Zlnka was somehow more not okay What was he doing here how long had he been committed He breathed and inhabited only this moment there was no past or personal background when he stepped from one room into another any record of occupying that space vanished too no footprint no residue The others they all spoke of nothing but themselves every inconvenience a calamity all the world's suffering localized in one fuckbrained vessel But we he and I talked of everything but ourselves This was how we passed our days It was the healthiest of all possible relations

ALL THE WORLD'S MONSTERS

People were out with their animals I'd left my sunglasses at the house and though that was the worst thing that could have happened I'd not make the error of *turning back* I'd not forfeit what small gains achieved and consign all to hell and shadows But without prophylactics how would I fare against the afternoon genocide As the first test one came impending up the sidewalk tethered to some minor beast No it would not go well I'd never gotten it down the pleasantries smiling like you mean it Yes good day to you as well may your children contract syphilis and end their days howling alone in an empty room Well what would you do Something normal I suppose And right away the first trial already flunked I spotted another just ahead one more bland harbinger of entropy I simply couldn't no more not again He stopped to let it pee here was my chance I swerved off the walk and cut across the funeral home parking lot I did this all the time but now there was a twinge of guilt as if using these solemn grounds as a shortcut somehow disrespected the departed and their mourners It passed soon enough I recalled that in the event of my own perishment there'd be no proper service casket headstone the like Who would pay who would come I didn't care about all that *ritual* anyway why so much bother A better idea toss me in a pile of wood chips and be done with it no rites no sanctimony finished and finished and green green green

1

It was a short walk from the inn Except the ice cream shop most places were closed a smattering of people about Over there the visitor center and there the police station a pale light glowing through the glass doors Four cruisers parked in front The sign in the café window was flipped to closed inside the two teenagers were sweeping and stacking chairs I sat on a bench in front of the library The sky was clear and there was a breeze and every few minutes a car would pass through the square The voices now to my left were the two café workers they'd finished for the night They crossed the street and entered the park passed through the gazebo came out the other side A cruiser had pulled away from the station Its headlights panned across me as it rounded the corner I'd noticed them earlier on the other side of the square the young couple coming up the walk now They glanced at me at the same time a hiccup in their conversation He gave me the nod men give other men I did not return it They moved on and resumed talking more hushed than before

The cruiser came back around and parked in front of me
I squinted in the lights He came up and asked for ID I
took it out he held it under his flashlight What was I
doing Out for a walk *getting fresh air* Had I been drinking
No Was I carrying weapons No Be careful He returned
the ID and left

I walked back toward the station No one was around
Three cruisers were in front now two sedans and an SUV
The SUV was closest Its number was 337

2

I couldn't tell the difference between people who lived here and people who passed through They littered the floor and sofas the four or five of them asleep in the front room Most fully dressed shoes even Because I didn't recognize them I pegged them as *passing through* although that wasn't a reliable criterion I mean the fact I didn't recognize them Many passed through Waves of flotsam Sometimes for a night sometimes days weeks They were the same They had the same stories the same smells They all chased after aversion as if that were a thing you could touch

These were the house rules *No jerks No hate Avoid injury to others Clean your mess Don't steal Respect the premises Use common sense Create freely*

It wasn't so hard to believe I'd open the door and find not the expected hallway but a dead relative's staid living room or the damp boys' bathroom from primary school When I got up the door appeared distant the room had turned oblong against its essence Another scenario was the door would open to a room that belonged to this house but hadn't been there before impossibly situated between door and hallway Familiar things were never familiar But I turned the knob and it was there the dim hallway Peeling wallpaper rows of closed doors Behind one voices and an acoustic guitar in tandem a bout of carousal toppled into dawn That it sounded to be waning meant I might live

3

Will doesn't change anything

4

He wanted to explain how it had come to pass that's what he said come to pass His name was Krn maybe Youthish withdrawn didn't talk to anyone Krn's voice was weak and halting you had to strain to hear All were surprised because none had heard him speak before near catatonic he'd been on arrival It was inevitable I thought that the others would get bored and start talking over him But the voice gathered confidence and for now okay he had our attention

Krn grew up in a poor rural home with several other children some biological siblings others adopted or under foster care He wasn't sure his father was his father His parents took in as many kids as possible to *milk benefits* he said and while some received preferential treatment most lived in an abject state of neglect never enough food new clothes unheard of Social workers were a fixture and when a visit was imminent they would hastily get the house into shape send a few kids to stay with relatives put the others in nicer clothes which were taken back after the inspection Children were sometimes removed only to be replaced by others Krn said the father had abused him in various ways as far back as he could remember His mother knew about it it'd even occurred in her presence He believed the other kids were assaulted as well why would he be singled out but he'd never witnessed it or heard anyone speak of it The children did not bond they were fearful guarded aloof Krn knew he was gay from an early age before he understood that word and what it connoted for many in the world around him and his first experience the first consensual one happened when he was eleven It was with an older foster kid he was around fifteen The liaisons continued for several months They were careful to conceal their activity sometimes meeting in the dense woods abutting the parents' property one time it happened in a cornfield Krn developed intense feelings for the other boy feelings he knew were unreciprocated He believes now the foster kid wasn't queer he was someone for whom the ability to extract gratification from another person any person was an end in itself As Krn's obsession escalated his demands for attention became more brazen and the older boy naturally retreated Thoughts of self-harm and suicide burdened his days It was inevitable the father would begin to suspect the relationship and one day he confronted Krn violently Within weeks the foster kid had disappeared and Krn never saw or heard of him again He was convinced the father killed the boy and buried him somewhere on the property though he acknowledged there was no evidence By high school Krn was acutely asocial unable to make friends let alone perform the awful rituals of dating Stunted and frail he wore mismatched secondhand clothes that didn't fit making him a target of ridicule He performed poorly in class and faced constant rebuke from impatient teachers Soon he was placed in a remedial track where no one cared enough to bother with him Krn felt disgust for his own queer body and increasingly sought ways to harm it He focused in particular on the offending organ he would make cuts in it and rub dirt and debris into the wounds which resulted in humiliating ER visits followed by brutal harangues from the father The first suicide attempt came at fifteen when he ingested a bottle of bleach Another ER admission this time followed by a long-term hospital stay after he developed pneumonia and then a stint in a juvenile psych facility By this time the parents' abuses and neglect had been discovered and all children were removed from the home and Krn soon found himself in nominally better circumstances the only child in a middle-class foster home Material comfort however did little to elevate Krn's self-concept and his morbid and self-destructive tendencies became more than his new family was willing to burden He was subsequently shuffled among foster homes rarely staying in the same place more than six months

His first experience with a girl the only experience he said happened when he was seventeen She worked at a movie theater he frequented a place where he found solace Every time he went she talked to him and people *girls* never talked to him She flirted though he didn't know what that was or how to gauge it could not comprehend that he might be the object of such behavior Despite everything Krn's nonresponses his annihilated affect the girl persisted She was older twenty-one and had an apartment One day after a movie she invited him over it wasn't so much that he assented as he lacked the apparatus to decline Such pliableness an impaired ability to say no facilitated his later virtual enslavement to wealthy older men The girl said to follow her to her car and he did so because he could not do otherwise Krn said he'd thought of trying to enter the straight realm that his eviscerated self might be mended by *normalcy* At the apartment the girl led Krn to her room and got undressed He had only seen naked women in pornography and even then he was mostly looking at the boys She didn't look to him like those women She lay on her back on the bed with her knees up and Krn noticed the unfamiliar smell and he wasn't sure what to do She told him to undress he did and she said to come to her She said to eat her pussy Eat my pussy Krn kneeled between her legs he was soft he still wasn't sure what to do He moved closer and coughed The girl sat up pushed him onto his back and put it in her mouth Once it was firm enough she straddled him and after some difficulty stuffed it inside No more than a few strokes and he shot into her It was a joyless spasm he said he didn't understand how *that* could be *incorrect* but that's what it was he said

A dark spot formed where his light-blue pants parted It streaked downward and drops fell from the cuffs and pooled on the floor under the chair Krn went silent and crossed his legs leaned forward and folded his arms over his lap Oh Jesus some person said and that's all it took The others fell into collective grumbling never mind that many had likely soiled themselves intentionally or otherwise in the recent past Krn got up and fled The session ended early we returned to our rooms

5

Tomorrow I was to meet with Jnlxo at the hotel I'd never seen or spoken to him and wasn't sure he existed Mrznr had arranged the meeting I don't know that he had understood exactly what I was after but there must've been enough information the right *keywords* for him to peg Jnlxo as the right agent He refused to put us in direct contact at first said it was not possible dangerous even so instead a series of puzzling dispatches was transmitted verbally via Mrznr I doubted for a while anything would come of it but a meeting was finally arranged at the hotel in the city where I'd been staying the past few days Mrznr being an inscrutable sort could have been setting me up I didn't doubt it but I didn't worry either because nothing mattered The deal was Jnlxo would arrive at my room at seven and I'd have to show him the cash before we proceeded any further The item wasn't even that expensive but became more so with what I guess you could call black-market markup a portion of which would no doubt go to Mrznr I gathered I would pay a lower per-unit price were I to buy in bulk but that would've meant looking much further ahead than my small mind would have allowed

You didn't chat you weren't friends Mrznr was there because you wanted something his reason for being Literal purpose not the other kind most everyone else has Mrznr didn't want to know *how I'd been* He hadn't known my name either I was sure of it as it should be But that was before I solicited other services that made identity unavoidable I didn't worry though because I'd never owed him money Before all that he'd been one more entrepreneur one among many in the marketplace someone to call on when no one else came through In that way he was peerless immune to the supply fluctuations that hobbled all the others He had connections they didn't so it was said and much was said of his hidden orbit and its trade in blood and fun and of threats and retaliations I knew some of the targets most were harmless there was no rationale arbitrary always But even with the occasional messy incident *you're not welcome here* said no one at any establishment ever They were fearful he was immune How was any of this my concern

6

The map was a disordered sketch of dotted and dashed and multicolored lines that ran jagged and serpentine across the sheet I could hardly make sense of it but it appeared to suggest that if I kept heading the way I was heading I would circle back to where I started There were trail names and sites of interest and icons denoting exotic activities Exotic to me at least because I'd never *hiked* in my life Nevertheless I had picked what looked like the longest trail A footnote warned of exhaustion and *challenging terrain* And why you might wonder did I even bother with this vile sprawl of disordered misery I wanted *immersion* I guess and *circularity* that was nice too but I had no illusions I fully expected to be punished I had no sense of it of what you do or why but it was something you did out here who was I to dismiss it And how bad could it be *these people* do it all the time But let's be clear it wasn't that I wanted to understand them What could be more facile than understanding

7

At eleven I left the inn and walked to the square The day was mild and beautiful the township thrummed with activity An old man sat across from me in the gazebo He had remarked on the fine weather and I had nodded and he hadn't said anything since Sometimes every few minutes I looked up from my book and toward the police station The car the one I was waiting for wasn't there yet When that became tedious I wandered around the park and watched the birds

A couple walked up to the gazebo *He* was on the phone telling someone to come meet them at the park One of their children if the condescension in each word were any indication Or maybe *he* talked to everyone that way *Her* face suggested as much A grackle alighted on the gazebo railing it pecked at something and rattled and clacked before flying off It was not hard to picture the brains coming out of *his* ears

My first visit to the township I had planned to ride until they told me I had to get off or until a place looked less drab and barbaric than the last place The bus stopped for a break at the station which was not a station but the cramped office of a local cab company doubling as a station Some trotted off in search of snacks or toilet or they *stretched their legs* or smoked paced talked on the phone or stood blank outside the bus and did nothing I looked around and decided I wouldn't get back on Did this place meet the criteria was it less drab and barbaric than the last place I didn't remember the last place so much for criteria I started toward the town center The sidewalk was recently set all level no cracks or pockmarks no sprouting grass between the segments I passed no house less than a century old all lawns sculpted and no people no pedestrians in sight anywhere After half a mile a shift from residential to commercial a realtor a law firm a teahouse

8

In the dream I had died but could still interact with certain people aware their numbers would diminish until finally I could communicate with no one though I persisted among them I roamed the city with acquaintances exes childhood friends We were solemn and spoke little no reminiscence no heartfelt sentiments or farewells much the same as in *happier times* Each fell away one by one I woke up before the last person became inaccessible The dream's gloomy residue carried over into waking awareness an added stratum of sadness on the day

Morning found the breach where the red quilt tacked over the window had been pushed aside Someone must have grazed it on their way out A bright shaft entered the gap and things maladapted to light were overexposed like the two plastic crates stacked next to the mattress dirt packed into recesses a long hair trapped in a sticky spot where something had spilled a black ant creeping along the bottom edge The crates were stuffed with magazines papers books a board was on top and on top of that a glass of water a knife a set of keys Purple blotches stained the unfinished wood There were other blemishes impressions as if struck by a hammer probably struck by a hammer nicks ashy burnt places Light glinted off the unfolded blade and the smudged white walls dotted with jagged holes were uglier than before uglier than last year or yesterday

The things you hear The serial beeps of a rumbling heavy truck in reverse And cars a thousand million humming toward sites of quotidian dread Shouting and jackhammering Kids waiting for the bus These unknown hours they were a calming jolt a pacifying sickness Outside was all frost and chill inside heat and oppression My mouth was intolerably dry yet reaching for the glass of water seemed not worth the effort

A pale metallic odor curled through the house I located its source an empty pot on the stove The heat was still on underneath it a memory of evaporated water Cups and bottles and cans crowded the kitchen surfaces I located a mug and rinsed it out Shutting off the heat on the stove wasn't my business I decided

The house rules were often modified sometimes in response to incidents other times according to the caprices of longtimers A new revised list would then be taped to the refrigerator usually in the same spot scrawled in the same black marker as if it had always been the same list If any democratic mechanism existed here it was invisible to me Most rules were risibly self-evident as if to imply all rules are suspect But that would credit the authors too much *Use common sense Avoid injury to others* No these were not formulated by a pranky ironist And what of the oblique ones the short-lived *Be neutral* Just as well *Be not Be no Be none* At one time *No hate* had been elaborated into myriad *-isms* and *-phobias* but these were finally condensed into the unitary directive mainly so the list would fit on one sheet Likewise *No jerks* Did anyone follow all the rules There are questions of interpretation What do you mean for example by *common sense* Yet there was one that was violated always by everyone and that was *Create freely*

I picked it up off the night table The handle was inlaid with multicolored wood set in a recursive diamond pattern The brass bolsters had become dull with age It was a gift from another life That's not metaphor I was someone else The whole thing looked dirty and expired now if such objects can be said to expire It was recently sharpened though and isn't that what matters I ran my thumb over the unfolded blade touched the tip a few nicks but yes still sharp It was sturdy and heavier than it looked and it was serviceable

9

Things and how you see them The former do not bend
to the latter

10

The asst marshaled me into the queue with the others dim
bodies trailing through the bright common area Many in
pajamas some clutching thin blankets about their
shoulders A few wore the familiar blue paper smocks
others conspicuously overdressed as if this were the day
the diagnostic error that routed them here would be
discovered followed by hasty discharge a fanfare of
apologies and retractions Some were shoeless wearing only
socks others in slippers no laces anywhere Half or less
than half were washed and groomed others dirty and
unkempt The latter remained that way much of the time
and the human odor was ubiquitous It was warmer here
than what most would find comfortable   The line
advanced as efficiently as could be expected no outbursts
as if there were tacit agreement that *crazy* was not an early
morning affair but a timbre best saved for later eleven
thirty or noon The ones who slugged down the decaf
shitwater I don't know what they were after did *they* even
know maybe they hoped for a placebo I didn't touch it
Some of us are placebo resistant we can tell when the
thing's not there

It has to do with a pinched face and closed body this unapproachability cultivated since birth Not talking helps too Kids didn't sit next to me on the bus teachers didn't call on me It sounds ideal I know but then you take unseenness for granted and forget someone might notice when you talk to yourself or pick your nose And isn't that the problem Others noticing and forming a *representation* of you   Lucky for everyone *that* phantom remains inaccessible always Because what knowledge could be more horrible than that Because who wants to know what anyone else *really thinks*

No outside food or drinks allowed

The kitchen worker an erstwhile patient said nothing didn't look at you There was an egg-like puck some gray mush a wedge suggestive of fruit Used to be visitors could bring in food subject to inspection but no more and that was fine I didn't have visitors wasn't eager to be reminded of what I was missing I sat at a corner table by myself Zlnka wasn't around She didn't ask if she could sit and it was okay at first she *wasn't there* which is the most you can hope for We inhabited our oblivions and ate and avoided It would have been much the same with Zlnka But words came out of her now threats and profanities murmured at some spectral adversary *Excuse me* I almost said but caught myself I wasn't the target she was looking off in the other direction why investigate why interfere The puck tasted better than expected How is it you know when someone is standing behind you You don't But I turned and Madi was there scowling Madi Zlnka had said was an athlete recently admitted because of an *unspecified incident* While locked in seclusion he covered himself in poop and fought with all he had when security came in Such studied commitment to being as difficult as possible inspires and edifies They were all afraid of him the staff you could see it He made some sounds at me What was it he wanted my spot my food an arbitrary altercation I said he had mistaken me for someone who would do what he said and he pulled me from the chair and tossed me to the floor They tackled him within seconds He got injected and was carted away The woman had left I finished breakfast

11

The trail was muddy from recent rainfall I had to maneuver around large menace-filled puddles and washed-out places It was humid and hot and gnats buzzed around my ears Only a few minutes had passed but I'd already excreted more sweat than ever in my life My punitive expectations had been exceeded Yes good more of that It became apparent my shoes were as unsuitable as possible and jeans likewise proved uncomfortable What else would I have worn I hadn't thought to bring insect repellent or sunscreen or water or snacks Nothing in fact except the map tucked in my back pocket But I slogged on anyway because an aversion to discomfort is incompatible with life Yes all you deranged Pollyannas things are always far worse than you think Yet that understanding did not foster stoic acceptance did not quell the thought it might all be better burnt to the ground Other conclusions were possible Some rot about *natural beauty* and the therapeutic benefit of time away from the built world Worse than *wrong thinking* these notions are categorically antihuman

12

It was disheartening the familiar tropes all there as if learned from movies This one spars with a hallucinated foe that one believes a demon inhabits her gut another's married to a pop star who's coming to rescue them There was sometimes a novel delusion or ingenious self-wounding but otherwise it was sameness and predictability The schizophrenics had poetry at least but isn't that cliché too

He belonged to none of the *categories* his presence made little sense Zlnka and I talked despite having few *common interests* Did he have *interests* Not in the received sense They belonged to no class of things never linked never unified We had *the game* yes and that mollified us but there was something more A common sense of life I can't articulate it His absence unsettled me It was not like him to miss things He understood the merits of affecting an interest in structure as a precarious benchmark of wellness

Not much to do for the two hours after breakfast no sessions or activities a good time to reflect on your wretchedness contrive ways to circumvent safeguards note the lapses that might allow for escape recall every wrong turn in life convince yourself you belong here stare at walls or worse at the large screen books were available but curated which meant nothing worthwhile it didn't matter I couldn't focus the sentences decomposed words became beads of black mercury and rolled across the page it belonged to a larger process of unlearning where I would become not only illiterate but also infirm unable to feed or dress myself nothing like the *treatment-resistant* long-termers who inhabited their preferred worlds with totality who must be distinguished from those who'd merely had a *bad moment* who were often of a repellent sort phony shits from moneyed families who expected *the best possible treatment* if only the maniacs who were never getting out anyway would target *them* it was the method that set me apart its statementmakingness plenty of scarred wrists here some bruising about the neck but many opted for ingestion with its built-in safety net to hell with them do you mean it or not all the safeguards in place on the unit they enlightened me about myriad self-wounding strategies I had never considered none of it mattered I'd no *intentions* here the problem with the whole enterprise was a failure to understand self-ruin as a logical response to life

13

Where everything is revisable facts are unwelcome

14

Lithe bodies smartly dressed summery and casual They drifted up to the gazebo progeny in tow A lovely day here in the middle They were everywhere and you couldn't help but imagine what sanitary horrors in the bedchamber Had it even happened in the last five years since offspring two No but he did commerce preschool teacher on the side and one day clocked Spouse so hard they had to engineer a story no one believed but pretended to believe to *save face* One supposes these things to have happened They continued toward the ice cream shop a trail of breezy scents

He was likely sleeping as old men do The one sitting across from me in the gazebo in the bright early afternoon The broad sunglasses made it impossible to discern But twenty minutes had passed without sound or motion A contrast to the surrounding whir of life

ONE WAY→Form Single Lane It was posted at the other end of the crosswalk for the benefit of traffic entering from Market Street Past the sign a red-brick path with two tall gray lampposts at the entryway followed by rows of green park benches The path terminated at the white hexagonal gazebo at the center of the grassy park Trees shaded the whole area Sculpted hedgerows flowers drinking fountains birdbaths Sunny and warm it was Saturday midafternoon People perambulated the square queued up at the ice cream shop on the southeast corner They browsed books set out on tables in front of the library at the opposite corner It was all familiar now On the northeast side the township police station next to town hall People idled about the park a man tossed nuts to squirrels Yelling kids ran through the gazebo and jumped around and scurried off

It was a painting of an alien The archetypal form with a triangle head and big black slanted insect eyes It was posed as a saint robes and all nimbus about the head right hand raised in holy gesture the slim index finger extending upward The painting was right there when you walked in mounted on the wall opposite the entrance you couldn't avoid it Another one was displayed prominently on the right wall It depicted an otherwise bucolic landscape but with three flying saucers suspended over a pond and barn against the afternoon sky They were a neutral fact of the scene as much as the rolling clouds lush treetops and blank-faced sheep standing in the grass I felt sick Don't they understand we're all alone that the whole predicament was a big accident All this before I reached the counter It was a cramped airless place the café next to the library The two teenagers working there were bored they slouched and made idle chatter They were unguarded in the way of parochial communities unlike the city where people gird themselves against the world's awfulness Right away they pegged me as an alien too albeit of another kind Was it so obvious what tipped them off They inquired where was I from what did I do what brought me to their serene anytown The glimmer of flirtation threw me off *don't you know better* It was boredom and youth and that was all I said I was from some other state and worked for a historical preservation society I had come to survey a site that had applied for protected status My job was to assess its condition and eligibility An older resident would have easily caught the lie but they simply nodded and made serious faces

It had not *aged well* the sound that pulsed from the speakers and polluted the atmosphere Also it had sucked to begin with The two workers obviously had no say if they had it would've been differently bad The café was stuffy and bright There were too many tables too close together It was hard to walk between them hard not to back your chair into someone else's Worse was the intrusive provincial gossip The place was contrived to repel anyone hoping to stay more than a minute or two So when my hand shook as I moved the cup toward my mouth I ascribed it to the miserable environs even though there might've been other reasons A couple sips and I left On the way out I bumped into a cop coming in He made a face that was all

But where to go A place that was not the café I continued past the library and exited the square After a block on the right a featureless brick building no sign I could see a shop perhaps one that needn't announce its scope of activity and shouldn't they all be that way a standardized code on

the front nothing more it would mitigate the vulgarity
The door was open Inside no customers and no one at
the register Maps and brochures were stacked on tables
and shelves along with mugs bumper stickers silly
decorative objects Some regional histories a guide to sites
of interest I picked up a map unfolded it the township
was smaller than I had realized A woman appeared behind
the counter and welcomed me to the visitor center She
was genial in a way that counterpoised my own depravity
I tried to refold the map clumsily forcing new and
unnatural creases until it obtained something of its original
shape albeit utterly corrupted Is this your first time here
Are you enjoying your visit Can I help you find something
No chimeric autofictions this time she was immune to
bullshit so I mumbled a response and bought the map
She thanked me Come back if you need anything else
On the way out I noticed a postcard a photo of the gazebo
and the surrounding park the township name imposed
over the top in a gaudy font The picture was enhanced
the grass and vegetation supernaturally verdant the sky a
richer blue than any I'd ever seen bright fat clouds that
leapt off the surface I turned toward the counter but the
woman had disappeared I tucked the postcard inside the
map and left

15

The showers were occupied so I went back to my room
I adjusted the red quilt over the window The foul
residuum of the last person I had shared the room with
still tainted the air It's likely I only imagined it but the
fact of its imaginedness made it no less potent That person
had only lasted a few weeks before it became necessary to
apply pressure The intuition that someone had to go was
among the few functioning aspects of this arrangement
My head pulsed I thought of the people who drill holes
in their skulls to cure their ailments what's the word
trepanation it even sounds insidious

Some kept a jug at their bedside I didn't care to but it
meant I had to go back out there No longer vaccinated
against the dawn the people in the front room were awake
now torpid and soundless I didn't ask directly when they
planned to leave and there was no reason for them to go
right away but I was sick of people so I asked whether they
knew Adlbr or any other resident and by implication what
association or agreement sanctioned this occupation of
our sofas The ceiling fan chirped as if it might dislodge

and fall to the floor or catch fire My socks felt damp I realized I was standing in a wet spot on the carpet and hopped to the side No one answered and I wondered whether I had said anything I went through the kitchen toward the back A heavy winter coat hung by the door a large pair of boots on the linoleum below I put on both Neither fit well loose too much bulk The back porch was long gone a four-foot drop now and cause of occasional injury or laughs We'd built a wooden ramp but it collapsed I leapt from the threshold and tottered on impact The ground was still moist from recently melted snow the whole yard a boggy life-resistant brown patch enclosed by a chain-link fence that sagged and bulged in places There were no trees a primitive fire pit was dug in the middle Toward the back there was a shack about ten by twelve where people sometimes lodged during warmer weather Tall messy shrubs lined one side I stood there partly concealed by the bushes facing the building's one window Inside propped against the wall an unfinished painting of a figure in a rowboat on a lake There was a crate full of records a mattress shelves with jars and boxes A hole in the floor you could stand in I'd spent many humid summer nights in there chasing cancelation with like-minded others Last summer sitting on the mattress with two strangers I thought this could be the night but morning arrived as it does A white plastic bag caught on the shrubs and quivered in the wind

I walked around the side of the house past the overflowing trash cans and stacks of soggy flattened cardboard boxes and out to the front yard a flood-prone muddy depression with sparse islands of grass An inoperable van was parked in the yard Orders to move it came often accompanied by allusions to impoundment penalties eviction these went in the same receptacle as most other notices Its owner had moved out long ago and the van had since been annexed as an auxiliary bedroom The mail wouldn't come for several hours but I went to the end of the drive and checked the box anyway The thought of seeing my name printed on something aroused both dread and a sense that I might be a person

It wasn't because of any change on our part but the complaints had tapered off A rich family had bought the house across the street a couple years ago and deposited some snotty little scions there The new occupancy coincided with increased cop visits notices citations the usual efforts to pressure us off the block Built into the hillside the house was a trilevel polygonal structure with a clerestory roof The outer walls were faced with irregular jagged stonework Attached to the south façade was a stone archway with a terra-cotta eagle perched on top it opened to a set of steps leading up the hill The architect had lived there until his death He'd built other houses in the area a series of late-career oddities As his posthumous fame soared so did the value of these weird buildings no matter the hard-to-access entrances or unlevel flooring But why the recent silence They were still there the ludicrous cars still came and went light still glowed in the clerestory windows People like that don't acquiesce they find new tactics One day I entered the basement when nobody was home Not much was there some building materials window screens antique doors stacked on the floor I did find on a dusty workbench in the corner one of those old manual hand drills the kind with gears and a wooden handle and knobs The gears were rusted but still turned I considered going up the steps and seeing if the door was unlocked I took the drill and walked back across the street

I went in through the front door and tracked mud across the carpet I returned the boots and coat to where I'd found them Bazdr was hanging out with the others in the front room He had lived there longer than me and could get on with anyone which made him insufferable Sounds came from the bathroom down the hall an agonized retch a deathly cough No one took notice I felt like doing the same but it was life sickness more than anything else The heaving would cease for a few seconds then resume I started timing the intervals A full minute elapsed maybe it was over but no it picked up again more tormented than before What if they died in there That would mean a battery of personnel in the house and all the nuisance and anxiety that would go along with it and still I'd remain unshowered But who was it Adlbr who was usually up before anyone else was conspicuously absent It would've been unlike him he was an ascetic and as out of place here as one could be Yet he had an unflappable tolerance for the asinine a refined stoicism which made him the ideal housemate The death rattles stopped and someone who was not Adlbr exited and idled up the hallway toward one of the bedrooms not the gait of a person who'd just nearly perished I sprinted toward the bathroom and locked myself inside They had left the seat up hadn't bothered to flush A painterly splatter of red-orange puke The tub contained several inches of murky standing water dotted with white flakes dermatologic lotuses that proliferated across the surface Long black hairs stuck to the sides There was no time to try unstopping the drain it would have to wait until another day or until the water reached the top and spilled over it wouldn't be the first time I got in and ran the water it was lukewarm so it had to be quick It was and I hastily assembled myself in a way I supposed met the rudimentary criteria for being in the world And then out into the obscene day

16

It was funny because in case you'd forgotten what a dark evil morass you'd flung yourself into in case you were less than vigilant there were plenty of signs to remind you *Beware of snakes Watch out for bears Stay on trail Caution poison ivy Warning cliff edge Slippery rocks Swift current* You spend millennia bending the world to suit your needs reordering the basic awfulness of nature to make it hospitable in opposition to all the pointless blooming and birthing and feeding and dying only for some jerks to come along and deliberately put themselves at its mercy and call it transcendent The best I could say was that no one had asked for change or to use my phone And no bristly beast had made lunch of me yet Could it be it was *not so bad* No I'd not allow it

17

They were still there The night table and the set of keys
on top The glass of water the knife The world had not
fallen away Already the sickly stirrings of morning
Correction would not bring peace

Too high and too far left it had penetrated the chest wall
and pierced the lung but missed the heart *Pneumothorax*
a word I remembered A major vessel avoided by a
centimeter I'd made a sound awful enough to raise alarm
no small achievement at the old place Someone found
me and made the call Supine with the knife handle
protruding paraphernalia all about the place And not even
finished How humiliating Did someone snap a picture
With luck it finds its way to an album cover or PSA
Coming to bandaged and intubated in the hospital there
was neither relief nor disappointment just embarrassment
I only wanted *more* Meds would have to do

18

Some of the people you know A few of them Many of them They pass their unremarkable days toeing the pit's perimeter with a diminishing resolve to resist its dark allure Everyday madness abounds We reject therefore that the commonwealths of sane and unsane have uncontested borders We see the sad resilient practitioners strain to find things that work and know it is lost

19

There was something worse than listening to them talk about themselves yes it was talking about yourself

Respect other members let everyone speak don't talk over others do not yell do not disrupt do not become violent stay for the whole session if you must leave don't come back participate listen be honest don't judge be spontaneous Most were violated every meeting except the last one Some sessions were structured focused on a single topic such as strategies for functioning in the world or pretending lifelong indigence is not inevitable   The information was useless for those who would never resume or begin *normal life* For the rest everyday functioning wasn't the problem we were unhinged in covert ways not readily managed and that we could *get by* made us all the more treacherous The staff got it but proceeded anyway as if following a manual as they certainly were one devised by a cabal of boring occultists barricaded in a dreary business park

Thus the shitshow of group

She was confident it would have a productive outcome It would be an open format where members could steer the discussion Perhaps when she awoke this morning rising well before the snoring mass at the other side of the bed and winced from the ache in her legs as she stood in the predawn gloom and shambled toward the bathroom and then downstairs to pound two cups of shit coffee she looked outside at the icy sidewalks and decided it would be a good day to court disaster Because life wasn't hard enough already

A malignant former acolyte had infiltrated the unit to fuck with Jord Here's how she knew On her way to breakfast a stranger had stopped her in the hall He looked like a person possessed of purpose she said which is never a good thing she said *The sacrifice of time* the stranger told her *has its profit in the destruction therein and with sincere worship I arrived at the ritual of activity and fuel of its emanation but it then turned sour and became a difficult paradox requiring magical effort to restore synchronicity* Jord was shaken Before that her day had been just fine The group leader asked her to consider saving it for her one-on-one so someone else could speak but Jord waved it off and continued A stranger she said could not have known about her dark power over the universal subconscious and the worship that had arisen from her synchronicity with television No it was a clear sign The infiltrator was a heretic an apostate She was frightened because now that she had relinquished her *dark power* for the alternative of stability she was vulnerable to malicious agents The leader tried again *I know your beliefs are very real for you and I understand your fear and frustration what can I do to help you feel safe* This pablum didn't get far with Jord she shot it down quick if they wanted to help her feel safe she said they'd expel the infiltrator and stop spiking her food with chemicals that made her feeble and compliant I wanted to stand up and applaud But then a new member someone who didn't know a goddamn thing told Jord the stranger's comment probably meant nothing at all that there were certainly no *infiltrators* in the hospital and they weren't putting anything in our food He was close enough to backhand Jord screamed and threw her drink at him They would get to him eventually if they hadn't already she said He could've been one of them for all she knew she said

Jord stopped talking Was she satisfied the meeting was sufficiently disrupted Or did she have a *moment* and step outside of things The latter must be hellish I'd seen it before Better to have no idea to inhabit a state so totally no other perspective is possible Much like everyone else in the world

20

For all I knew his name wasn't Mrznr And I'd no idea
whether he'd ever procured a fake ID but who else would
I ask If he couldn't help he knew someone who could I
hadn't seen Mrznr since I got out of the hospital He
always held court at the same spot on the same high-back
barstool of cracked red leather his throne of blood but I
didn't want to just show up without getting in touch first
So I did and that was where he said to come the usual spot
It had to be a professional forgery no shoddy thing made
on a cheap home printer and laminator Except my words
didn't come out like that instead some stammering
paraphrase next to him there at his end-of-bar perch all
menace and business as ever Yeah no problem Give him
a few days That was all Had he done it before who knows
but where there was potential for commerce Mrznr would
not likely demur *For all I knew* he'd done this many times
But as promised he got back a couple days later he needed
a photo some information The amount was less than I'd
expected though I hadn't known what to expect It didn't
matter Money found me one way or another and I gave
half up front

At the spot a couple weeks later we reconvened and he handed it over Better than I'd expected *though I hadn't known what to expect* and I gave him the rest He threw in a bag a nice packed-full one a dispatch of goodwill from a charred corridor of his bombed-out heart Someone came by and placed a heap of hot food in front of Mrznr

21

The station at night is a black affair a layover for exiles
and miscreants adrift in the demimonde Maybe it's not
like this everywhere I'm sure it isn't but here it's like this
A mugging in the restroom an abandoned infant a
runaway trying not to attract attention Always a story
contrived to relieve you of a few bucks There was nothing
especially lurid on this night someone crying on the phone
another talking to themselves someone else hassling the
staff A group of stranded migrants The bus to the
township was usually no more than half full and tonight
was the same It was easy then to sit far away from the
bad-smelling person near the middle A body in its natural
state is a loathsome thing The ride was tolerable no yelling
or fighting no acknowledgment from anyone

22

It was a languorous Tuesday night in the township The place was empty The bartender was bored she wanted a story she said Naturally I began to think of exit strategies of excuses pretending to have dementia whatever it would take to get out of there But okay fine I said To improvise well requires practice

When I came around I said she was alone Mother a high-school dropout without skills a refugee from the country of steady work and Father narrowed to a couple candidates a matter best left uninvestigated Relocation was frequent brief stays with family members or friends or boyfriends that often came to an abrupt end things packed in the middle of night or tossed to the curb in the middle of day Memories from that time are dim though certain indiscretions are salient There was the one time more than one time they knew I saw them but they carried on anyway And that one like most of the others he treated her badly yet in his case she let it continue longer than usual Faint impressions of discomfort the scent of chlorine a revolting dampness yes I believe she let him do those things to me I understand the vagaries of memory and I'd not want to accuse spuriously but it might help explain the difficulties later on Eventually she settled with a certain one and I suppose there was calm for a while He was *fond of drink* weren't they all and there were the bad nights but we had food and rent was paid and thus it was better than before Marriage followed and I received his name and soon more children arrived I wanted nothing to do with my half siblings and did my best to avoid them By nine or ten the aversion to everyone and the troubled behavior started to cause concern at school She and he pretended not to notice even after the youngest half brother sustained an injury causing permanent impairment in one ear Little was done aside from a half-assed effort to not leave me alone with the other children There were other things It didn't become a particular habit but I was not always kind to animals and later around twelve there was some trouble when I masturbated in front of a younger girl from school Far more incidents went unreported I had learned that certain threats will keep most kids quiet Things deteriorated between her and him This was during my early teens He was increasingly absent she was increasingly drunk and high me and the others were hardly looked after The two youngest half siblings were placed with a relative and soon afterward she made a half-serious suicide attempt and was gone for a short while When she returned there was a limp quasi reconciliation between her and him The two younger children came back and so did the patina of normalcy The first time I was fourteen It was a large family gathering at a state park mainly his side since she had little contact with her family most of whom lived far away I had set off into the woods with a younger cousin about seven or eight With so many people around no one noticed our absence There was no plan I was just bored but deeper into the forest it tugged at me a still-nascent appetite without a name Coaxing her to the cliff edge was easy she was trusting and obedient Even then it wasn't completely formulated but intuition took over and I pushed her off A brief cry a thud on the rocks below next to the stream No need to look I returned to the camp area and some time passed before anyone noticed she was missing Things transpired as they do Realization followed by panic a frantic search of the campgrounds everyone calling her name contact the authorities search by helicopter eventual discovery It was ruled accidental the child had wandered off unattended the parents guilt stricken over their negligence If anyone suspected me it was never mentioned no one put it together that we were gone at the same time After the first time you realize how simple it can be and it sets you on a prescribed course The only reason more people don't choose this path is the pivotal opportunity didn't present itself Happenstance is key Everything you see and hear they try to chalk it up to a fundamental disorder usually in tandem with a set of sociological factors But that's not it I mean it's not reducible to that Any ordinary person given the right circumstances could do the same The next one happened a few years later and in college it became more frequent It's a skill like any other you figure out the best tactics develop efficient habits learn from your mistakes Do I worry about being caught It doesn't crowd my thoughts It will likely happen one day Many fantasize of this life Don't for a minute suppose I'm the first to have passed through here the first you've served or had a conversation with

Each time I stopped to do one she refilled the shot glass I'd lost count Her reaction to the story wasn't what I had expected though I don't know what I had expected Not a skeptical word or gesture all interest no shock It's a hallmark of the trade a knack for concealing your estimation of people but no the signals were there her interest was sincere Even if she were bluffing and planned to pick up the phone right after I left I'd shown her the false ID used the fake name hadn't mentioned where I was staying She didn't ask many questions except of all things she wanted to know about Mother's suicide attempt *how I felt about it* I said I was deeply affected which I realized was not entirely consistent with the rest of the narrative We talked until after close All kinds had passed through she had stories of her own she said She invited me over An inchoate hesitation collected enough mass to obstruct an immediate response but I remembered intuition is as unreliable as anything else

She lived with her father who was *away on business* The place was nicer than I thought it would be We went to her room where there was a tall cupboard of old heavy wood She unlocked the top doors Inside the shelves were filled with bags and containers of different sizes bricks of black plastic Hundreds of thousands of dollars' worth of stuff perhaps There were weapons too I had shared my *secret* so this was hers She took out a bag and locked the cupboard The next couple hours were spent chopchopchopping on the solid oak dining room table

There was talk and more talk as there always is and as always I remember none of it We did make our way to bed and that too is banished from memory It could be that nothing happened Most likely nothing happened In the morning she drove me to the station Along the way we didn't exchange a word What was there to say The familiarity established the night before had evaporated along with all stories and all secrets all vanished

23

Behind the counter in the narrow gray office a wide man was on the phone yelling at someone I was an hour early Cabbies came and went jabbering and complaining I unfolded the map from the visitor center the silly postcard fell in my lap The township sat at the fork of two creeks that ran along its northern and southern borders It occupied one square mile and had sixteen hundred residents at the last census The square lay at the center The map showed five churches one major grocery store a funeral home a preschool primary school and high school along with various businesses mainly concentrated around the square There were several banks far more than seemed necessary for the slight populace wouldn't it be better to have one centralized body to manage that particular affliction The station lay outside the township limits suggesting it served the surrounding area not just the township It was hard to imagine the town itself would need more than a couple cabbies I folded up the map I got it right this time and tucked the postcard back inside

24

The point is I could not have done otherwise That probably sounds nonsensical I had not been coerced at gunpoint or threatened with blackmail but here's what I mean It was *because* the township was situated in the highlands *because* there were forests and parks and campgrounds that it was inevitable I would *go hiking* It's what you do Choices rest within a larger order of things where the choice to *not go hiking* would have been a false choice would have meant yielding to a different gravity one equally outside my control *No you had a choice* You don't understand things at all you idiot

25

Fifteen minutes before departure she flared into the
waiting area and sat down a bulging duffel bag slung over
her shoulder Ghostly with long sleeves against the season
she drew up her legs and lay her head against the wall
closed her eyes After a few seconds she repositioned and
tried again to rest There were two or three of them
nickel-sized purple spots on her neck exposed when she
pushed a tumble of hair behind her shoulder Was this
only a stopover a scenic dip between points of shadow
Perhaps she was a local who went out into the bad world
and returned damaged only to be shunned and shuttled
away She could've passed through the old house for all I
knew On the afternoon bus back to the city I sat as far
away as possible

26

For a couple blocks there was nothing it was quiet no cars even   As if all had been decimated by an unnamed something another dumb novel sprawling suburban tracts left in situ a flatiron burning a hole through slacks eggs crackling on the skillet All these places were uninhabitable anyway I couldn't imagine Eternal labor servitude just to keep up with upkeep there are worse things one supposes yet nothing suggests itself But ahead at the next intersection resilient life in evidence you can't keep a good invasive species down crowds flanked the street families children perched on shoulders elderly propped in lawn chairs Why loiter in this cold on purpose don't you know what time it is shouldn't you be at your lousy job or school or arrested-living place The whole mob was oriented in the same direction but toward what Again something eschatological no doubt you can't keep a good resilient invasive species from also chasing after extinction so what now burning chariots swarming locust a river of blood roiling down the avenue under a blackening sun Maybe I should turn back But hark the approaching clangor of drums and horns And there it was A parade of course it too a herald of the end times This is what I missed sleeping half my days The procession was just coming into view when I reached the intersection the crowd stretched several blocks In lieu of any practical detour I'd have to wait for it to pass Smiling people in some manner of costume stationed on floats waved mechanically bored children wearing colorful hats some stared open-mouthed at the scrolling crowd forgetting to smile or wave a fire truck rolled by then some cops on horseback Unending balloons The theme eluded me what occasion what justification a holiday perhaps the kind I dependably forget until I realize there's no mail service What better preparation for collapse than pointless celebrating

I turned down the alley A tall wooden privacy fence ran along one side the backsides of some businesses along the other A few cars were parked there no people in sight The expected alley stench The dumpster I was looking for was the one behind the café It was usually good for some bagels or still-edible fruits and pastries or recently expired premade sandwiches There it was about halfway down the alley a stately blue thing *Caution do not play in or around dumpster Not for public use Area under surveillance Do not block Unauthorized vehicles will be towed* Still no one around I lifted the lid and looked inside Not much there no usable foodstuffs I could see Was it trash day had someone beaten me to it had they not taken anything out yet What I did notice was a thick paperback book on the bottom I climbed in and retrieved it some minor dirt and discoloration but no ripped pages it wasn't wet still readable I wiped it off and took a closer look The book was several hundred slightly yellowed pages of small print The cover announced it was the *Principia* of Berko the Elder

Inside the café a cyclorama of the sartorially homogeneous hunched over devices or reading or talking Dinky minds crackling and bleeping that pernicious strain of stupid peculiar to the young and educated Were their parents awful too I noted how well they complemented the art affixed to the maroon walls unremarkable local stuff Oh but wait ha-ha *unremarkable local art* that's redundant right I guess they were all parade-averse as well and I guess no one had ever told them to shut up I tossed my satchel on a table in the corner I went up front and ordered I returned and opened the *Principia* to the Introduction

> Little is known of Berko the Elder Born in a remote area of the South Desert about 400 years ago he was orphaned when his parents died in the war After a period of wandering during which he reported having ecstatic visions in a state of severe deprivation he was taken in by a colonial family who nurtured him and saw to his education The remainder of his life is said to have been spent largely in monastic seclusion occupied with the work of composing the *Principia*

You see I wasn't *eavesdropping* That would imply agency where there was only nonconsensual reception Over at the next table they were unflagging and gesticular and it must be exhausting I thought to be always indignant It's not about the interlocutory content per se which is frothy and fungible You can swap it out shift it around mince and dice The problem is they are all still *interested in things* and unceasingly *right* So it was inevitable my gaze would sloom toward the place where that one's bare upper arm connected to their shoulder and also inevitable I would imagine intercourse with that part and all that would entail logistically and otherwise

> There are no confirmed portraits of Berko He left behind no papers or effects only the magisterial *Principia* About seventy-five years after Berko's death a purported biography appeared Culdex's *Life of Berko* Among its many unverified claims is that during the Interim Troubles the young Berko ten or eleven at the time killed one hundred settlers armed with only a sling and a club Not long after its publication the *Life* was deemed a hoax its author a known pederast and opium smoker

I know telepathy isn't real So do you But then *but then* they reached around and they scratched the back of their shoulder *the same shoulder* a deep prolonged four-fingered raking as if a caustic irritant had been slathered there And I was forced to consider for a moment it might be real Aghast at my own treacherous brainspace I recoiled and retreated into the book

I learned apocrypha aside there is agreement Berko's style is a deliberate parody of a better-known philosopher of the time For example

> The only way to build such cooperation that will defend them from despotism and the injuries of powerholders and thereby secure them such that by their own industry and the fruits of the earth they can nourish themselves and live contentedly is to invest all their power and strength in a community or network of communities that may fairly render all their wills by direct participation into consensus without coercion which is to say to form a cooperative or assembly of cooperatives to bear them

> where everyone freely agrees on actions decided by the
> collective in matters that concern the common peace and
> safety and thereby find their will expressed by the
> assembly and their judgment by its judgment

And then it went down the wrong way The tepid stuff
I'd been drinking And no matter its essential unboldness
it caused me to start coughing like I was tubercular
Everyone in the café noticed and all around there was
horror and pity but mostly horror and you could see the
half-formed thought limp across their darling faces *Should
somebody do something* The universal will thus aligned in
my disfavor these paroxysms had the added calamitous
effect of triggering my very earliest memory That's right
the birth memory my nativity my *error* and the
disappointment attendant upon it Gasping in the sad gray
world I thought my best days are behind me the future
will bring only failure infirmity death Already I was
prescient When they cut the cord I sighed and said *it must
be nearly finished*

But the hacking fit ended finally and the origin memory
dissipated along with it Delivered now from the onus of
caring about the well-being of another the habitués could
all return to being solipsists

So saith Berko

> This is more than consent or concord It is a just order
> of free individuals in a network of voluntary associations
> made by a covenant among all participants such that each
> says to each I agree to equal participation in this assembly
> or assembly of assemblies on the condition you agree as
> well without compulsion and participate in like manner

> When this is done the multitudes thus united in free spontaneous association shall be called Harmony This is the generation of the great stateless society or to speak more reverently of the specific good to which we owe our peace and our defense under the universal good

She came by and gathered some crumpled napkins from a recently vacated table next to mine and wiped it down Straightened up the chairs returned the condiment caddy to its original position She threw away the dirty napkins took the lid off the trash can pulled out the full bag and tied it off hauled it out through the back door She came back and emptied another receptacle that was near the front Maybe I'd check the dumpster again The day was opening it became abruptly sunnier and the whole room brightened

> By way of this free constitution comprising all participants under a state of Harmony the community has legitimacy and efficacy such that by means of mutual assistance it can orient the will of all toward peace at home and direct action against coercion And within the collective consists the essence of Harmony which is a community whose actions are authored by each member of the great multitude through mutual covenants In this way Harmony may use the strength and means of all members as it deems expedient for peace and common aid

When she returned to the register a man was there waiting I had noticed him earlier noticed his *gait* his *angularity* Taut skin over high cheekbones It was no surprise then that he had a *grievance* It didn't matter what it was they're all the same Everyone stopped and watched while he dumped his harangue on the woman behind the counter

She said nothing back because it was her job to receive abuse It was over however before it really began as he soon gave up on whatever redress he'd hoped for and marched out into the cold bright day She took someone else's order the room returned to status quo

In my head it went like this

I picked up my satchel and left I hurried toward the narrow parking lot at the side of the building Only one car in the lot could've been his and there he was walking toward it No one was around I crossed the lot quick to catch up to him before he got in the car Excuse me I think you left this He turned like he was going to tell me to get fucked But then his face changed maybe he did leave something behind I reached into the satchel as if to retrieve the lost item *You left this inside* In one immaculate motion I closed the gap between us pulled out the U-lock and caught him across the face with it A crack and he went down gurgling for help spitting blood and teeth

But that's not how it went The man drove off his jaw intact I stood in the lot He looked at me through the car window a faint contortion in his face I dumbly watched him pull into traffic and speed away I couldn't bear to go back inside now all those mouthbreathers and me no better In time they will become him *Principles* will decompose into careers and investments creature comforts vacations endless policies you wait and see Under the early afternoon sun I slunk across the lot no idea where I might go What would someone with responsibilities do

27

Tiny frogs hopped off the path as I approached My foot caught on a truculent root and being of *unsound structure* I collapsed with sudden violence I was left with abrasions muddy clothes a reconfigured ankle One less acquainted with *fallenness* might capitulate but no I persisted like a freighted witless beast unaware it's a few paces from expiration I limped across creeks and streams on narrow wooden bridges stopped and took respite on a bench near a waterfall Exhausted already my chest thumped as it normally would at 6 am after a fun fun night of fun No this wasn't for me and I regretted everything that had led to this point And wasn't it strange I hadn't seen anyone else on the trail There was the mud yes but when did that ever keep *them* away Did they know something I didn't they almost certainly did Settled somewhat by which I mean restored to baseline anomie I got up and continued along the trail

28

She adjusted her bifocals and squinted at it No one had
taken a second look until now I stopped myself from
correcting her when she spoke the name next to my image
now It was an upmarket inn I'd chosen mainly for its
proximity to the square A mistake probably but after the
ruins that had been my base in the city the week before I
wanted a reprieve It would be the final night there would
be no others I might as well be comfortable The inn was
a former private residence that had been converted after
the wealthy owner's death I didn't know until I got there
that there were only eight guest rooms I'd never made a
reservation in my life It turned out a room was available
a rare coincidence are you sure you want it more affordable
places are nearby yes I want it and she excused herself and
blustered off to an office behind the front desk Muffled
consultations behind the closed door Adjacent to the desk
was a lounge with a fireplace and a screen above it showing
a news program Paintings on the walls of animals and
children warm subdued light it had the estranging comfort
of someone else's living room A couple guests loafed on
a wide brown leather sofa in front of the fireplace They

had structure and a place in the world they had thoughts about the news The desk clerk returned and said I could have the room but it would require a substantial security deposit cash only I put the bills on the counter and her face tightened She sighed the sigh of someone who'd spent a lifetime sighing and slid the key across the counter Enjoy your stay

I ascended the wide heavy-wooden staircase to the second floor Elaborate stained-glass windows shining antique hardwoods in the hallways I already missed the crummy hotels so familiar I'd become an appendage of the architecture Where were the vending machines the noisy icemakers stale murky corridors with grimy carpet and garish wallpaper a prostitute and client behind one door a junky huddled behind another a body behind that one perhaps But *here* I was an imposter who had infiltrated an extremist organization where any moment I might be found out and tortured and shot I turned the key an actual metal key and opened the door A queen-sized bed a couple chairs a writing desk a mounted screen No minifridge or coffeemaker but plenty of ornamental bullshit some tepid landscape paintings functionless decorative pillows I set the duffel bag on a chair took my shoes off got on the bed A tall headboard of thick wood finely carved posts at the foot An antique light fixture overhead I thought of the colorless people who had laid their heads here and dreamed of golf

Hotel bedspreads are not washed between guests

I switched on the screen and clicked through until I came to an animal program A coiled black snake a mamba the voiceover says is squeezing eggs from its underside When it finishes there are fourteen eggs Cut to ninety days later the baby mambas are emerging from the eggs One extends toward the camera and opens its mouth all black inside the tiny fangs visible in the roof Their venom glands are fully developed at birth the narrator says the twenty-inch newborns already equipped to kill a human We follow them as they leave the den and enter the world to seek prey I turned and emptied on the floral-patterned duvet and wiped on one of the decorative pillows The show had ended it was now a mysteries-of-the-deep program

29

I need to talk to you about that thing That's what someone had told me to say Go up to him to Dehmeck at the bar and say that It was as ridiculous as it sounds and I was ridiculous doing it but the ailing dignity could not repel the virus of need so I did as I was told and Dehmeck gestured me toward the end of the bar *What do you need* he nodded it more than said it I gave him the bill and he put the thing in my hand Easy enough That was a few years ago Now we were better acquainted and could dispense with code and innuendo We could be marginally less ridiculous I say better acquainted but I knew Dehmeck in the way everyone in that milieu knew each other which is to say not at all though we carried on otherwise Or better I knew Dehmeck not at all the same as no human truly knows any other He had just opened I was the only person there And that was good no opinions or nonconsensual talk scant evidence of life It was too early to start piling on the enhancements and besides it was gauche to hit up Dehmeck before six or seven or eight thirty No just *the usual* and I'll gird for the long afternoon nothing The warm spreading mist the unqualified good that is a comfortable stool in an empty room

Doing it alone is best but if nothing else the presence of another helps validate your choices So when she lurched through the door and mounted the stool next to mine the initial panic soon eased into baseline discomfort She heaved a bulky purse onto the bar and motioned for Dehmeck and ordered a double something or other She'd come from another spot down the street she said I'd been there once but never went back because of the repellent clientele I tried to explain that but it came out wrong The other place had cut her off for being soused at such an indecent hour Dehmeck's was a refuge for such souls you could stay as long as you liked provided you could keep your head up and place a coherent order She talked more and I nodded I couldn't do small talk but that was no impediment since she was happy to fill in the gaps and iron out the awkward bits When I say little time had passed I shouldn't be trusted but after *little time had passed* after shots and loosening intentions emerged The hour was indecorous I motioned Dehmeck over anyway

There was never much joy in any of this The pleasure flash and then what The desperate blank wide as waiting

We retreated to the bathroom and locked the door Filthy with graffiti all over the walls a single backed-up toilet a cracked mirror I fished the bag out of my pocket and unsealed it with my thumbs I dipped a key into it scooped out a mound offered it to her Pressing one nostril she snorted it into the other I dug out another for myself She resumed a monologue she'd begun at the bar After finishing high school she continued she was accepted to a small liberal arts college far away from home Her father resisted stressing she should attend an affordable local college and pursue a practical course of study In protest she opted out of college altogether and didn't speak to her father for the next four years During that time she worked a series of service jobs had several brief relationships marked by increasing dysfunction went to a lot of parties Further litanies of familial discord resentment toward more ambitious siblings perceptions of preferential treatment by the parents She didn't say it outright but I gathered she still received financial support from her family I realized I had laughed or smiled during parts where it was not the expected or appropriate response I keyed out another she took it and I leaned in and kissed her She returned to her story and I perused the graffiti on the wall behind her The usual profanity sometimes a single word as if that were sufficient to proclaim the author's soul crude drawings of genitals statements of unfiltered bigotry She broke midsentence and asked for more We had nearly emptied the bag She got on her knees and fumbled with the front of my pants I resisted at first this rarely turns out well there were *side effects* but then I remembered the things that make life bearable and relented The worst happened as it does but this only caused her to redouble her efforts Recalling her story I admit had bored me earlier I now found I admired her obstinacy against her father's stifling prudence not to mention the disregard for propriety that would find her in the present circumstance She moved with ease between the noisy world outside and this hidden sphere of activity well versed in the customs of both Her efforts were effective and I swelled causing her to momentarily gag Overcoming the reflex she started again working faster I soon burst and she moaned approval took time to ensure I was emptied She got up straightened her clothes glanced in the broken mirror Her demeanor had changed she even declined a final lift She thanked me for helping her *feel like a whore* those words exactly opened the door and left I lagged in the bathroom splashed water on my face smoothed my hair did some more When I came out she was gone In her place some new customers whom I resolved I would sit as far away from as possible I hung around another hour or two didn't talk to anyone

30

After the blast the husband fell beside me with obvious head trauma A lone chunk of shrapnel had traversed the considerable distance between the gazebo and the station and had found its target as if foreordained to do so There were sounds of cars crashing Alarms Screaming The wife who was uninjured crawled to him oh god somebody help I was still crouched on the gazebo's wooden floor Smoke and dust billowed across the park I pulled a shirt out of my duffel bag applied it to his massive bleeding wound it was no use a part was missing but I told the woman I'd get help The old man who seconds earlier had appeared to be asleep was standing now looking disoriented In front of the station the burning frame of cruiser 337 cars nearby damaged and on fire as well Smoke surged from the station's blown-out façade bodies and body parts lay about the street and sidewalk The explosion had also caused accidents among cars driving through the square one had veered into the park plowing over the one-way sign and striking a couple pedestrians I could see them now prostrate on the grass People were getting out of their cars running toward the wounded Frantic phone calls Shouts and wailing

31

All memories are bad memories

32

The lugubrious mornings before service Gray skies and a light drizzle a mild chill it's always that way in memory although it couldn't have always been *that way* He was never not there standing outside a thick cigar in his mouth its odor curled around the drab red-brick building over the shrubs and down the sidewalk I hate cigars

He'd had a vision of the afterlife a dual revelation he told us He began with inferno and that was fine because it was sure to be the more arresting of the two But this was no fiery pit of horrors no frozen lake with a gnashing beast at its center In his revelation it was a banquet hall so vast you couldn't see from one end to the other A site of unequaled decadence the hall was assailed by the golden light of a hundred thousand grand chandeliers Elaborate candelabras were affixed to the walls candles eternally lit The centerpiece was the immense dining table that stretched the length of the hall Larger than any table that could exist on the earth it was made of a heavy dark wood with intricate carvings in the legs and edges The table was lined with plush armchairs also made of finely carved wood and it was arrayed with every dish imaginable all the world's cuisines represented equally all displayed on gold serving ware The resulting olfactory swirl evoked the pulsing horde of all cultures extant languishing or extinct Naturally the damned were all seated at the table One might be tempted to regard this as more divine than demonic more reward than punishment But that would be a mistake for all those sublime dishes were situated just out of reach of any *guest* of the banquet Moreover the spirits were all chained to their chairs preventing them from climbing onto the table Each sinner was furnished therefore with an enormous utensil several feet long so he or she could spear or scoop the distant victuals There was a flaw however Once the desired item was attained there was no way to get it back to your mouth The hall was only wide enough to accommodate the table and chairs so if you tried to move the fork or spoon backward the handle would simply knock against the wall And attempting to maneuver it in any other direction would invariably produce a melee of clashing utensils or worse you'd bash it into another guest at the table The food would likely fall off the end anyway Some spirits hadn't the strength to lift the oversized wooden implements at all Malnourished and emaciated each wretched soul starved in perpetuity with an exquisite feast right before them There were no *servers* to take plates away and bring new ones that unlucky caste found all it could want of hell in the terrestrial realm yet the dishes never expired and hot foods never cooled It was unsurprising then that in their frustration and wickedness the condemned assaulted each other with the hefty utensils causing hideous injuries Eyeballs popped out of sockets cheeks torn open dangling skin flaps exposed teeth and gums Some had been stabbed in the chest with the massive fork permanently lodged there The stately table the fine chairs the marble floor were all awash in blood and viscera Eyes hunks of flesh teeth scalps and gristle All the shades at the great table moaned and wailed without cease filling the hall with a ghastly music

He turned then to the revelation of paradise Heaven he said was identical to hell in its arrangement the same grand banquet hall the same endless table holding all known dishes and all the rest The difference was that unlike the hideous spectacle of debased sinners in eternal conflict heaven was a tableau of harmony and compassion in which the blessed did not attack their brethren but used the great utensils to feed one another No one starved no frightful wounding all were joyful and content in their ceaseless feasting There was no need to fasten them to their chairs because all were altruists acting in the best interests of their fellow pious souls

We groaned we felt tricked What had we expected I don't know Puffy white clouds and gates of pearl white-robed angels plucking at harps vast mansions where reside all the saints walls encrusted with precious stones white horses clopping down streets of gold the eternal light of the Lord no darkness no night But instead we got a drab moral lesson To this day I think of it and curse his name May his cigars rot a hole in his tongue

33

By my estimate which was no doubt completely inaccurate I was about two-thirds of the way through I entered a more dense area of forest where the tree cover blocked out the sun It was cooler and less humid here the insects less invasive and the ceaseless birdcalls sounded more placid and less like shrieks of horror If only the rest were like this I came to a well-maintained boardwalk which I could see not far ahead led to a large wooden platform that jutted over a ravine It was the largest man-made structure I had seen on the trail so far It was hexagonal similar to the gazebo in the township square about the same size in fact with railing on all sides except the opening There was a sign *something-or-other overlook* I didn't recall seeing it on the map but mine was a life defined by an aversion to noticing things I got closer and there for the first time since I'd begun the hike I saw another human or humanlike disturbance They were standing at the platform's end There was no one else they were alone I'd no sense of what matters of etiquette might apply but I decided to wait until they left to go out there myself Meanwhile I tried to quash the unease ignited by encountering another lone hiker

Blinking in the bright lights I stood outside and looked through the tinted storefront windows It was a few blocks south of the square I'd somehow never gone this way before The people inside were striking balls with sticks on felt-surfaced tables they made faces as if they were doing important things Between shots they poured drinks from pitchers and talked and laughed Two couples tumbled out the front doors a gush of smoke music voices They swayed up the sidewalk in the direction I'd just come from I thought I should keep walking but instead I went inside It was too much at first the bustle and life but I got used to it I bought a drink and found an open table Inept in every way I'm sure but I watched what others did and tried to do the same racked the balls then jabbed at them until things went into holes When the table was clear I gathered them up and repeated the dull ceremony After a few cycles of this a guy came up and offered to shoot some games with me I would guess we were the same age I said I'd no idea how to play I was bored and seeking distraction It didn't matter he said he wasn't any good either it was a way to pass the time to *hang out* He had a relaxed disarming manner if he'd been some other way I would've found an exit before the first break *Okay* We played a few games had several rounds on his tab His name was Tam he had lived in the township his whole life his uncle was the mayor He worked at a bank he was recently divorced One of those was a lie I thought It didn't take long Even I could tell he'd deliberately missed some easy shots he held the cue in a way that betrayed greater skill than he let on What did he want A relative of his an aunt I think worked at the inn where I was staying he said It was no doubt the same woman who'd given me a hard time but I didn't mention it And there he did it again this time an illegally pocketed eight ball thus handing me the game Tam was trying to pick me up Was I flattered *Categories* are pernicious things aren't they If circumstances were different *Well* But this wasn't the night I was civil when he at last became clear thank you but no I'm sorry It was something more than this particular instance of failure the sadness in him it was hard wired Intrinsic The defeat of effort come to nothing and at no small personal risk it was not lost on me I declined as well his offer of a ride back to the inn and walked alone through the dark

She wasn't around when I got back to the inn Tam's wretched aunt if that's what she was I slipped away to the room and went straight to sleep The pool-hall encounter was replayed except this time Tam's overtures were not declined and we were here erections pressed one against the other on the floral duvet Tam in dreamworld had extreme preferences not anticipated by his social self It was messy business with poop and blood all over the upmarket room His uncle the mayor was there too in uncertain capacity Did auntie intrude as well We'll say she didn't

35

I'd get help for her husband I told her again Sirens and alarms now from all directions The truck was abandoned in the middle of the street near the ice cream shop driver-side door wide open One hundred feet give or take from the gazebo I picked up the duffel bag and ran that way and got in It was still running I maneuvered around other stopped vehicles around the people in the street and the debris and exited the square and drove toward the nearby highway There I turned in the direction opposite the direction that would've led back to the city First a police car then more police cars ambulances fire trucks in obverse beelining toward the township obverse to where I was going wherever I was going The polyphonic sirens a pleasing dissonance whirling screams and squawks but they were receding now So long The truck's owner must've been tall the pedals almost out of reach I felt along the side and found the switches the seat hummed forward Further manipulation and it lowered and even tilted the controls were sensitive and versatile Now I searched for the autocruise among the assemblage of levers buttons knobs on and proximate to the steering wheel there were functions here I didn't know existed After this and that produced only failure nothing intuitive everything obscure and was that the design intention the whole murky world writ small on a cluttered steering mechanism I hit finally on the right thing like everything else it was luck and nothing more and I set the speed to five over I put the AC on maximum which was only tolerable for a couple minutes The radio had been on when I got in and I'd left it going it was all sameness and rot but my attention had been crowded with other matters The broadcast was interrupted now by news of the blast so I searched until I found an oldies station it would do for now I exited onto the first interstate that came along Traffic was light gray clouds on the horizon I scanned the radio once more looking for the weather but most broadcasts were talking about *the thing* so I gave up and went back to the oldies station I was startled by a sequence of multipitched beeps from somewhere inside the cab an insipid tune made stupider by digital transposition I found the flashing phone it was right there in the console and I grabbed it and tossed it out the window threw out my own while I was at it I drove on at unfaltering speed on the straight and flat stretch of interstate almost as if not moving at all as if not barreling toward doom placated by the gentle duet of tires and engine On the passenger seat there was a brown bag of fast food It seems at first a benign thing but look closer and corruption and ruin are there I reached inside and ah yes some fries left on the bottom That they were cold hardly diminished anything

36

The stories you've heard they're all true Indignities great
and small atrocities howling demons If you were smart
you acquiesced Ego made into puree

Stringed instruments were out of the question Are the
reasons not clear Instead we banged on rudimentary
sound-making things or sang popular songs How did the
songs *make us feel* they asked If it's difficult to imagine
anything worse that's because there is nothing worse You
went anyway Other times we drew with crayons or made
biographical comics using stick figures When not pure
unreality the stories were pure negation and true to life
either way

Zlnka was there He didn't explain his earlier absence and
I didn't ask They gave us a lot of construction paper and
crayons tape glue tissue paper and children's scissors We
were to fashion a house-like thing maybe it was where we
grew up or if that was fraught with trauma and evil the
home of a relative or childhood friend even a place we had
lived recently Any place that was *pleasant* Okay I

wouldn't have to *think* at least and I got to work assembling from crags of memory a pale one-story everyhouse It was a dealer friend's place and it did not want for happy memories I cut out a big square for the façade a rectangle for the front door a smaller square for the front window and a large triangle for the roof and glued them all together Done in five minutes They came by and asked me to talk about it I did not falter It was my grandparents' house I had spent many lazy summers there I said They responded with something approbative and moved on One person had made a multilevel three-dimensional house with a yard and driveway it was like the home of a sitcom family Another's creation resembled neither a house nor any extant thing all the paper had been cut in curved or jagged lines and it was decorated with wads of tape and splotches of glue it was a mound or tower or pile And this one a simple A-frame structure a penis drawn in red crayon where the door would be and the chimney it was a dick too All were *interesting* they said Zlnka I don't know why had taken the task seriously He crafted several sheets of gray paper into cubes of varying size he used so many he had to ask for more and glued and taped them into a stacked modular structure It was how I imagined this building the one we were in might appear from the outside *Imagined* because I don't recall ever seeing it from the outside What was the word *brutalist* It too was interesting

He waved his dick at us and said faggots Zlnka and I who had just left the activity room He had flattened himself against the wall of the bright hallway palms and cheek pressed into the smooth white surface and he inched along in this manner pantless and free When he saw us he turned and it was there the turtleneck tip of it poking out from the bottom of his white shirt and that was when he said and did the thing There was no malice in it he expressed a fact as he saw it He turned back to the wall A couple of staff came up the hall one holding a pair of trousers They admonished him to cover himself and behave else he be placed on such and such restriction He did and they let him be Zlnka gave no indication he'd heard the man's remark or noticed the gesture What he did do was suggest that if we were to have a race with the man pressed against the wall us at our normal walking pace and he inching along where the pantless man was given a considerable head start we would never truly overtake him despite being faster He made reference to some *paradox* If only salient facts would blow right past me

37

Pergamon was an ancient Greek city and one of the great centers of Hellenistic culture It's no longer called Pergamon nor is it part of modern-day Greece It's a cluster of ruins in the western hills of some country But at one time it had many temples and palaces a bath complex a grand theater Zlnka took a bite of his sandwich We had a table to ourselves in the common area He continued The earliest references to Pergamon are from around the fourth century BCE At that time the city was volleyed between Greek and Persian rule in a string of battles Pergamon housed one of the preeminent libraries of antiquity it is said to have rivaled the Library of Alexandria with as many as two hundred thousand manuscripts Though it's possible some scrolls were transferred to other libraries most are likely lost It's astonishing to consider what unknown masterpieces or important historical documents might have been held there works that could've reshaped our view of that world or even altered the procession of culture The library fell into decline around the end of the second century BCE when following a series of unsuccessful revolts the city was fully conquered by Rome Pergamon was largely stagnant for the next couple centuries until the emperor Hadrian aiming to revitalize the city launched a succession of projects including the construction of an enormous temple that would become known as the Red Basilica itself part of a vast complex Rome was still polytheistic at that time and the Basilica was likely devoted to the worship of a dozen or more primarily Egyptian gods It is believed however that the temple was mainly dedicated to the Greco-Egyptian deity Serapis and in fact the Red Basilica is sometimes also called the Temple of Serapis But there is another deity that was possibly worshipped there The Egyptian bull god Apis We do know the temple contained a life-sized bronze bull possibly a representation of Apis It was hollow and the interior could be accessed through a hatch in the side Many such bronze bulls existed in the ancient world and while their uses varied the original purpose was rather specific In the sixth century BCE the despot Phalaris ordered the invention of a hollow bronze bull as a device for torture and execution Phalaris was no commonplace tyrant and during his sixteen-year reign in the Sicilian city of Akragas he is said to have committed innumerable atrocities including eating live babies But with the brazen bull Phalaris found an especially novel way to dispatch his enemies or anyone he found tedious on a given day The victim would be forced inside the bull the hatch secured and a fire built under the bull's abdomen One ingenious feature was that pipes built into the bull's nostrils would amplify the victim's screams mimicking a bellowing bull Among the many adversaries Phalaris had decrepitated inside the brazen bull was the bull's architect Perillos of Athens who for unknown reasons had run afoul of Phalaris And as if to provide an object lesson in the vicissitudes of history it is said Phalaris himself was executed inside the bull when he was overthrown by Telemachus in 554 BCE Other sources however say he was stoned to death by a mob of Akragan citizens For centuries afterward other brazen bulls were built and used for similar purposes One was even discovered among the spoils at Carthage and was rumored to be the same bull used by Phalaris As for the bull statue at the Red Basilica though it was no doubt used for devotion to Apis it also provided an efficient way to execute Christians as in the well-known example of Saint Antipas the martyred bishop of Pergamon The brazen bull remained in the Red Basilica until the fourth century CE when it was transferred to Constantinople where it became the centerpiece of one of the city's great forums Five major forums lay along the Mese the main avenue of Constantinople The Forum of Constantine Forum of Theodosius Forum Amastrianum Forum Bovis and Forum Arcadius It was *Forum Bovis* or the *Forum of the Ox* that housed the brazen bull from Pergamon Like all forums of Constantinople it was a public square that alternately functioned as a bustling marketplace and as a space for public events such as political speeches and debates Forum Bovis was also a place of torture and execution Countless unnamed Christians along with many well-known Byzantine figures perished there The deposed emperor Phocas Justinian's associates Stefanos and Teodatos Saint Andrew of Crete All broiled inside the brazen bull And so in between festivities and debates and the buying and selling of tunics and flasks many a martyr was made in Forum Bovis The bronze bull also made for a good heater as the season

warranted   By the time Constantinople fell to the
Ottomans in the fifteenth century no traces remained of
the Forum of the Ox Though its location is known from
the literature the site has never been excavated Today the
area is covered by roads and populated with commercial
and residential buildings hotels and shopping malls It is
also a known site of sex trafficking and prostitution No
remnants of the bull itself are known to exist and in fact
no part of any brazen bull from any period has ever been
recovered There are textual records and sketches and
paintings and nothing more

Zlnka stopped talking I was yanked from antiquity and
deposited back on the unit All the bad smells body smells
Did he even know what he was talking about

38

Unmoored from the hospital I had floated about the city the old house no longer an option Well it might've been an option but the situation had changed someone else had my room now Oh and the sour whiff of suspicion Shelter was offered out of obligation but these weren't the sort to come out and say it *you're not welcome anymore* Investigators had been nosing around giving them a harder time than usual because of me no doubt I'm sure that's what they thought I became familiar with lousy hotels shelters hostels I wasn't much anchored before but now there was nothing

It was an hour by bus to the township What did I do there Walk around the square browse the shops and galleries pass an afternoon in the library or café Lunch in the gazebo Most places closed in the early evening I'd either catch the late-afternoon bus out or stay at the budget hotel on the highway Or sometimes I'd stay with an acquaintance I hadn't planned on *acquaintances* but plans rarely went as planned A successful day was one not soiled by interaction no excuse me please thank you a horse's dick up your ass It's harder than you might think One way is to first wash and groom with more care than usual to *purify* which can also be preceded by fasting depending on your commitment to nonsense and then swaddle your vestal body neck to foot in good thick fabric well soaked in kerosene Try to light up in a place with steady pedestrian traffic In front of the thrift store or pastry shop Don't sit there like a pious asshole run around wave your arms make a show of it This will make it harder for some hero jerk to try and intervene And no one will ask if you're okay

39

Closer now and I got a better look at the person out on the platform Their back was to me and they were still but not completely still I mean a certain faint rhythm in the bent elbow a mild agitation of the whole architecture They or he a him yes that was clear now wore an odd hat and greenish-black assemblage that was not camouflage in the usual sense but performed that function I must've gotten close enough for him to hear my footsteps and he abruptly turned and there was no mistaking it now

As promised the trail ended at the beginning

40

The first couple days I dawdled in the shabby hotel room ordered delivery paced stared out the window at the parking lot The screen was never turned off Jnlxo wouldn't come until later in the week I still had the bag Mrznr had tossed in as a bonus

When you're messed up you think everyone can tell and some can but isn't it narcissistic to believe anyone would take such interest I trawled the convenience-store aisles implored whatever power binds the universe to spare me unnecessary contact It was enough that I'd had to shower back at the hotel And then the onus of dressing and opening the door and walking a couple blocks Any prepaid junk would do I bought the phone and got out of there

I had seen him earlier in the parking lot He was fidgety and skeletal and had the desperation Now when I came out he was standing by the door When it happens every day you develop automatic responses *no sorry* But this time I pulled out my wallet thumbed through the bills held out a hundred He snatched it from my hand I don't think the denomination registered He shoved the crumpled bill down his front pocket *Thanks* A nervous look around and he shambled off

It goes back centuries you see it in paintings and written accounts the practice of putting a mirror along the backbar behind the rows of bottles You can hardly find a place where you're not compelled to notice yourself always looking weary and unhinged it could be the lighting or the grime on the mirror but it probably isn't There are hypotheses about how this arrangement emerged and why it became standard but the most plausible one is never mentioned that the arbiters of temperance devised it as a way to shame offenders into moderation or at least burden them with self-loathing I was tight in the chest and in need of a foil The place was a couple blocks from the hotel and full of people transfixed by screens A few rounds and things were mitigated and it was possible to think again I took the burner phone out of its packaging It was like a toy I was surprised when the display lit up surprised such a device could be made so cheaply There is nowhere in the world to hide

I'd gone this way a dozen times but hadn't noticed the hardware store a few blocks from the hotel It was closed but thrumming with overnight stockers replenishing shelves with esoteric plumbing parts tubs of putty stud finders So the next day girded by twelve hours of deathful sleep I went there They all smell this way lumber plastics fertilizer that was my thought when I stepped through the wide automatic doors There is no such thing as a slow time of day here Everywhere perennial do-it-yourselfers scrutinized paint swatches and pipe fittings loaded lumber onto huge carts Locating common items was an ordeal and I was loath to ask for help but after some agony I found the things a soldering iron wire cutters magnetic strips Then the existential horror of self-checkout followed by the inevitable surprise when the alarms didn't go off as I passed through the doors

41

It was colder now it would be dark soon After I'd slipped
out of Dehmeck's bar I'd no idea what to do or where to
go so I found the nearest bus stop and waited Soon I
discovered I'd just missed the most direct line home the
next bus wouldn't come for over an hour I walked farther
than I would've liked to board a different bus that would
involve a longer ride at least I wouldn't have to stand
around in the cold The bus came I got on more crowded
than I was used to

There was an open seat near the back the only one I hated
it The whirring giant motor the jerking and shaking but
it was better than standing As ever they were there certain
as nothing is certain riders with no destination who
assemble in the back to avoid the ingress and egress of
people with shit to do One looked at me as though I'd
breached the sanctum sanctorum and I suppose I had But
the differences between us were negligible weren't they I
hadn't much to do either Yet theirs was a different sort
of world aversion mine self-imposed theirs less so The
bus stopped and more hurried aboard filling the cabin

beyond capacity doors clapped shut and the vehicle surged rattling ahead through the night I grabbed hold of a stanchion to keep from tilting into the person next to me The man in sweatpants across the aisle his legs spread as far apart as they would go he in effect took up three seats what an asshole

Finding no place to stand in the middle cabin she squeezed through to the back A glance at the near-uninhabitable spaces next to the man in sweatpants and she moved instead to an open spot in front of me I was still holding onto the stanchion she leaned against it and her hip bone pressed into my fingers Yank your hand away or say something or hope they will move I did not There was a sudden disturbance in the back row of seats a *sharp exchange* people problems it was over as soon as it started The bus hiccuped and lurched and she reached for the strap hanging overhead still mashed into my knuckles but the locus had now shifted centerward Minutes and nothing had changed I looked up she was fixed on the dark reflective window Another bus zoomed past in the opposite direction a scrolling filmstrip of solemn faces in the lighted cabin She got off at the next stop Did she intend to board another crowded carriage and do the same to another was it habitual or a fluke I hoped it was the former

Before I could get through more than a page they asked what I was reading I pretended not to hear but it came again from behind excuse me I asked what you're reading I did the logical thing and turned and waved the book around as if to swat away a hornet and then slammed it shut a limp gesture with a slim paperback They grumbled I couldn't understand much of it but this part leapt out you don't belong here And that was probably true in ways they didn't realize but still I turned and said why don't you shut the fuck up which surprised me as much as anyone else The person and their cohort went grimly silent My stop was coming up I had to consider now if I got off they might follow but if I stayed there could be trouble as well I reached into the satchel's side pocket and extended the blade of the box cutter

I got off at my stop No one followed or said anything and I was neither relieved nor disappointed I stood for a moment in the stinging cold it was about five blocks to my house I followed the main avenue for a couple blocks then detoured left onto a cross street The brick-paved road was quiet as usual The right side was lined with red-brick terraced houses and on the left older wood-frame homes butted against modern asymmetric agglomerations of glass steel and concrete The lights were usually out by ten Halfway down the street a running car was parked in front of one of the older houses its red taillights filtered through a plume of exhaust Even at a distance in the dark you could tell it was a police cruiser As I approached I could see the blue glow of the instrument panel illuminating the interior The car was empty which lent it a spectral strangeness like a screen broadcasting to an empty room Aside from the cruiser's presence there was no sign of anything amiss in the adjacent house I took a right and continued up the block A playground on the left a baseball diamond tennis courts Further along on the right there was a construction site that had been abandoned not long after the foundation was laid some time ago The neighborhood was littered with these perennially unfinished projects This one looked like it was intended to be yet another drab apartment building Just as well left unbuilt But now there was something new several pallets of bricks arranged parallel to the sidewalk at the front of the site forming a kind of barricade The steel-banded red cubes were beautiful in themselves in contrast to whatever vulgarity they would be marshaled to compose I plucked a brick from the nearest stack a three-holed type with pointed corners and well-defined edges Four or five pounds I gripped it in my gloved hand It fit well any larger and it would've been unwieldy

I circled the block arrived back at the corner where I had first turned off Up the hill along the main avenue clusters of light snowfall fluttered in the orange streetlamps I wrapped my scarf around the lower part of my face and pulled up my hood The cruiser was still parked there on the brick-paved cross street taillights still gleaming I hurried down the street and finding the car still empty I slammed the red brick into the windshield Where I had anticipated a snare-drum pop there was more of a thud I was rattled by the impact Cracks radiated from the jagged hole in the window like lightning Glass fragments sprinkled the dash and the black upholstery Still clutching the brick I considered taking out the driver-side window as well but thought better of it and ran

I cut through the narrow corridor between two houses crossed a backyard came out in an alley Ran more then slowed to catch my breath The snow was starting to accumulate Further down the alley I saw the back of the large church that occupied the center of the neighborhood I remembered there was a stairway in the rear leading to the basement When I got there I scuttled down the steps and tried the door no surprise it was locked I stood for a minute at the bottom of the stairs and started to uncover my face but stopped realizing there might be a camera A narrow rectangular window of wire-mesh glass was set into the steel door above the handle like a classroom door Inside I could make out a dozen metal folding chairs arranged in a circle on the concrete floor A whiteboard was mounted on the wall a column of black writing a list of some kind but I couldn't read it I backed away from the window and gazed upward along the building's rear façade past the enormous round window and steeply pitched roof and into the sky Sirens squalled in the distance I ascended the stairs the snowfall had abated I removed the scarf and hood and turned out of the alley followed the sidewalk up the hill Streetlights reflected in the windows of parked cars The brick was heavy in my satchel I took it out one corner chipped from its collision with the windshield I tossed it in the tall dense hedgerow bordering the lawn of a four-story house Up ahead a puny shivering dog had stopped to poop in the snow next to the walk I'd seen it before it was old it would shamble along barely able to keep pace with its owner I considered crossing the street but they were too close now I didn't want to appear *impolite* So I'd little choice but to stop and chat with the man with the shitting dog He was genial and contented lulled into smiling insouciance by the drooling familiar What were the sirens all about he wondered wherefore this breach of our peace A belligerent

jaywalker I suggested an aggressive squirrel who knows
His face became serious This guy was alright yet amid
some contentless gab about the dog the usual scenario took
shape in my mind There is an exchange of *sharp words*
improbable as it is followed by a *coming to blows* The
altercation culminates in me stomping his face into the
curb breaking half the teeth in his stupid head or maybe
causing an orbital fracture There were permutations of
this scene but its structure remained the same and as
always there was no reason for it at all I said good night
and went on my way up the hill A block ahead a cruiser
rolled through the intersection training its spot on the
opposite side of the street By the time I crossed the
intersection the cop was a safe distance down the street
and I was almost home I imagined the man with the dog
at the police station They're showing him dashcam
footage of someone smashing the window then fleeing
down the sidewalk There's a glimpse of the assailant's eyes
but the rest of the face is covered *I can't be sure* he says in
his neighborly way *he was not out of breath He seemed calm*

The house was quiet and dark The front room deserted
now the itinerants must have moved on to graze in
friendlier shitholes I went to my room and lay down still
humming from the impact Anxiety panic those were there
too I pulled a magazine from one of the crates No there'd
be none of that For the first time I noticed that a
concentration of holes and gashes in the wall resembled a
certain archipelago in a far-off part of the world I'd never
visit What to do when you can neither focus nor rest Try
not to think that's all

42

During the blank in-between hours when no one demanded my attention I would count the steps every step as I scuffed around the unit I knew exactly how many it took to get from my room to the common area or from the kitchen to the seclusion room It required focus and a deliberate pace I could also calculate how long these perambulations would take down to a few seconds barring any interference from some patient or staffhole It was a way to keep the sutures from tearing and letting the whole thing go swooshing to the floor The oddness of this habit wasn't lost on me I probably appeared indistinct from the others but why not assimilate More importantly it had the veneer of tradition It's what you do and wouldn't you too Yes you would because no place is worse than the city of thought in revolt

They gave me the wary looks who could blame them As if they knew I didn't truly want to join in I hate cards but a willingness to perform loathsome tasks is a good indicator of readiness to reenter society So when I passed the room and saw what they were up to I recognized a great opportunity to demonstrate my commitment to banality What I hadn't understood was the gravity of my request It was a place unfriendly to dilettantes and my imposturousness showed like a pox After the others had balked the one missing a quarter of his skull offered me a seat at the table The game I'd seen it before though I didn't know what it was Each of the eight players had their own complete deck of cards each with a different design Unlike others who seemed to know the rules a priori it was apparent I'd not have an easy time learning them But I tried and to the irritation of the others kept screwing up In my defense they weren't good at explaining rules There were no *turns* everyone played simultaneously as if conducting group solitaire cards were rapidly smacked down in separate piles at the center of the table players reached over and past each other lunged across the table one stood up and shouted at someone all of this in the normal course of play I followed none of it That I failed to grasp the game intuitively might be said to have boded well for me It ended abruptly with a clear winner a serial arsonist though why or how that person had won eluded me They gathered up their cards for the next round Mine lay undisturbed Before it began they all looked at me There'd be no *misread cues* they'd not allow it and I got up and left

43

Heading back to the hotel from the hardware store I tried not to notice things The world need not intrude more than you permit It was fine for a while but then at the next block a familiar something was crossing the street The same clothes same hat as the person I'd seen on the platform in the woods While the green outfit had made him part of the forest architecture here in the city he was anomalous and *unnatural* Crossing the intersection he glanced in my direction and there was nothing I was used to going unnoticed but I had cause to believe there might be an exception in this case In the bright downtown daylight everything looked different the sun reflecting off the ubiquitous concrete nothing like the trail shaded and cooled by the dense tree canopy Maybe it wasn't the same person Or it was but a person in one setting is someone else in another I even doubted what I'd seen in the forest It was too tidy this transposing of nature and unnature I had to consider the world would intrude as it pleased

44

They reminded me I was to meet with the Dr today I didn't know I was to meet with the Dr today I had seen him once for a brief assessment I panicked what could this be about how I should behave Too candid and I'll never leave too normal and it will look like a performance I knew better than to insist *I don't belong here* They showed me to his office It was spare no sofas or plush leather seats just a cheap office chair in front of a plain modern desk The same bright overhead lighting that cursed all other parts of the hospital I was told to sit and wait Right away I spotted all manner of *contraband* within reach on the desk A pair of scissors plastic pens paper clips a spiral notebook a plastic bag containing takeout food a glass of water Simple negligence or a provocation A setup Was security waiting outside the door to see if I tried to pilfer something I'd always entertained the idea I was under constant surveillance though it had never blossomed into actual belief Yet here one might reasonably expect to find unsound belief confirmed

I ignored the contraband and looked at the single art print

hanging on the wall next to the desk A human figure wearing purple and white vestments sits in a bright gold-yellow armchair with ornamentation at the top His mouth is open wide like he's screaming like he's trapped in the chair The whole image is distorted as if we're looking through a sheer curtain suggested by vertical striae traversing the painting Light streams from beneath the armchair in curved bars Is he being electrocuted is he someone with power It's silly to look at a thing as if there were a key to unlock it But maybe the Dr would explain it to me I looked past the desk and through the narrow window at the adjacent building's gray brick façade

The Dr came in and sat down and didn't say anything He fussed with some objects on the desk opened and closed drawers took a drink of water Tossed the bag of food into the trash He glanced at me and flipped through a notebook He stopped on a page adjusted his glasses and made a face Starting at the apex of his forehead the Dr's hair had retreated to form a slender peninsula the mainland a wavy mass that curled over his ears and covered the back of his neck Gray streaks had begun to proliferate He had large meaning-filled eyes with deep shadows underneath The whole face trended downward a resting scowl I thought he might be drunk

Many are *beyond help* as they say You know that For them *talking* about things certainly won't do any good That much is well established So we manage and palliate by the usual means until the story reaches its sad and pointless conclusion For you however some would have it that *working through* the accumulation of things that brought you here might obtain a certain efficacy that you could be nominally repaired if not truly fixed I'm not sure that's the case at all I would suggest rather that talking helps neither of us I nod reassure you maintain eye contact feign interest But I already know all the stories they're mostly the same and knowing those stories knowing your story your *iteration* tells me nothing about how I might help you But maybe *help*'s not what we should be after maybe we've got it all wrong You didn't come here seeking help someone made that decision for you Now you must accept help whether you like it or not And so you putter through cheerless days coaxed into brainless activities we both know are useless We talk to you like you're a five-year-old and in response you say what you think we want to hear Do you benefit from this coercive helping No It's obvious Let's say you're in a house that is on fire You can see the way out just ahead and if you hurry you're assured a safe exit Now what do you do Do you stand there and say I am not going to walk out of this situation until I've worked through the reasons Do you lament that you didn't replace the failing surge protector you knew was a hazard No you get out Yet we say to you the space you inhabit is dangerous it's dangerous to you and possibly others but instead of allowing you to flee we confine you to that space for as long as it takes to make the needed repairs Never mind that we're not even sure we've got the right tools or that we've correctly identified the structural flaws Meanwhile you suffocate When I said many are beyond help I didn't mean they cannot be helped that their condition is too severe for intervention to be of any use No Allow me to revise What I meant to say is that help is not appropriate it's *unsound practice* you could say yet within the scope of accepted practice unsound is normal and unhelpful help is demanded *Help* if I may posits that condition A is valid while condition B is not And what makes that the case You know the answer but we're not supposed to discuss it Let's approach it this way There are beliefs and the world is made up of those beliefs Not everyone sees it that way in fact most would have it otherwise There is the way things are they say and there is the way those things are understood and the two do not always align The latter is sometimes called delusion But what they do not say because that which is simple and obvious is banished is that what stands between the two is power The very spatial relation we find ourselves in right now me behind this desk and you over there vulnerable in a relatively less comfortable chair the status of this room as my office not yours this relation lacks balance and it is value laden In this relationship I do not provide a service you require like a plumber or hairstylist This is why my profession poses certain difficulties for me No that will not do What I mean to say is this is why I find my profession odious I am not a *mental health professional* that doesn't describe what I do at all it's entirely euphemistic There is a regime that sets the parameters of the human I am both architect and enforcer and you have a say in nothing I know what you're thinking Isn't this all a bit much aren't there perfectly good reasons for the whole apparatus wouldn't the alternative be a nightmare Or a worse nightmare I should say You're thinking of the deluded ones who count movie stars or heads of state among their closest friends people they say will send for them any moment and snatch them out of here Or those who have caused great harm to themselves gouged eyeballs mutilated genitals missing appendages And yes the classical cases those who hear voices talk to phantoms believe vast conspiracies are afoot someone's swindling them out of a fortune government agents are tracking their every move or manipulating them with radio waves Or maybe you're thinking of the psychopaths who are a danger to everyone around them who can only be managed through restraints and courageous doses of this or that The ones who slam their heads into walls the unyielding catatonics What about them you're thinking is not their illness their need for care beyond dispute You're correct and I'm a crank who should be delicensed But if you can bear with me a moment longer let's consider an example a *case* He was in his late twenties he'd been in and out of facilities for years The parents first took him to a specialist when he was in his midteens because of behavior they considered disturbing It became clear after talking to the family that they all believed he'd been normal during early childhood and had become increasingly abnormal over time Yet the specific features of this behavior *intolerable* they called it were never precisely explained I only knew that at some time in the past he had been good which shifted to bad and eventually mad You see where I'm heading Understanding these perceptions was as important as understanding the behavior itself They said for example he was an *easy* baby not troublesome and therefore good But we all know a normal baby is demanding and anything but easy which is to say the family saw deadness and called it normal On this view the later troubles are hardly surprising The norm-*setting* regime the family I mean took as *correct* deadness pliability a total absence of self-assertion and recoiled when not-dead conduct manifested and therefore sought intervention from a norm-*enforcing* regime In other words deadness is life and *life* is unreasonable You think this is an oversimplification that it's too tidy and obvious You should understand that obscuring the obvious is how civilization proceeds *Progress* you could say is proportional to how much distortion permeates all things a monstrous procession whereby the human becomes as abstracted from humanness as possible And where is your agency in this ineluctable process of alienation It's trampled by those who hold a monopoly over definitions it's disfigured and inverted until coercion is called choice So maybe you have an improved understanding of things now I've fulfilled a prescribed role and in some manner *helped* you Not that you're any better for possessing this knowledge no your exile will only deepen But as I said we must dispense with the idea that I'm here to help That's marketing *Propaganda* I'm here to eject clouds of ink I'm here to smuggle in genocide through a birthday cake

The Dr turned and looked out the window at the gray brick wall The mass of hair tumbling over his collar was ridiculous That's all thank you I glanced again at the black organizer on the desk and noticed I had somehow missed it before an antique letter opener with a finely carved mother-of-pearl handle Who still uses these I imagined picking it up and extending across the desk and plunging it into the side of the Dr's neck

I left the office There was no one in the hall I wasn't sure where I was no one was there to escort me back When they'd brought me here I was anxiety ridden and not paying attention I turned down the hall in the direction I thought we had come from Nothing familiar rows of closed doors I came to a set of heavy double doors the kind that usually demarcated a restricted area There was a reader on the side I assumed a badge would be necessary But the doors opened mechanically and I passed through to an area terminating in an elevator and a side door leading to the stairwell Did I want to escape I didn't remember taking an elevator or stairs on the way to the Dr's office Could I simply walk out I got in the elevator and pressed the number of what I thought was my floor Once there they had to buzz me through If they were surprised I was unaccompanied no one said so

45

Day's residue But now as I tried to *flee the scene* it was as if my ankles were shackled or feet burdened by boots of concrete Solemn neighborhood people like sentinels posted on their porches or lawns or in the street watched me struggle to put one foot before the other Despite the sense I'd been running or trying to run for several minutes when I turned the violated police car was only a few feet behind me The crowd *wasn't* encircling and closing in they were static a band of menacing garden gnomes but it sure felt that way and then *deus ex machina* the scene shifted and I was back at the basement door of the church But now a white light shone through the rectangular window and the steel door was unlocked Inside instead of an empty room the metal folding chairs in circular formation like a site of ritual were now occupied a dozen people in all They didn't notice me The whiteboard was still there on the wall but now a face was drawn on it with black marker It wore a dunce cap and had Xs for eyes A name was written under it and over the top it said you are only as sick as your secrets A person kneeled on the floor in the middle of the circle The others repeated the slogan written on the whiteboard and took turns spitting on the person Someone else a leader perhaps appeared and started beating the kneeling person with a belt Between strikes the leader would say a new slogan and the others would follow suit Soon all were speaking at once I took a few steps toward the circle but then there was the ringing from somewhere else and that was all

46

Every day people in a dismal state were shuttled back into the world Some returned within days or hours Others soon incarcerated or found dead Zlnka was exemplary but remained What criterion what checklist item It was all flipped back to front

47

She messaged around midnight said to meet her at the warehouse It took a moment to dislodge myself from the church basement I squinted at the message and reread it a few times I couldn't recall the content of any conversation I'd had with KD but she had reliable access to things thanks to a wealthy older acquaintance with whom she had an arrangement of indeterminate nature It's clear that total avoidance is unviable You have to allow for that But if we've no choice why *not* seek maximal utility

It was getting harder to distinguish between deliberate and spontaneous action I was already heading downtown when a version of that thought messily cohered and pushed through the murk and muck

The warehouse sat on a fenced-in lot along the access road of the interstate I entered through the back gate that was never locked Inside there was no sign of anyone it took a minute to orient myself in the darkness and locate the hallway that ended in the room where I was told I would find KD and her companions How this place had come to be occupied and repurposed was never made clear There had been some shows and other events but mostly it was all-night parties and rotating squatters It wouldn't last these places never do There'd be a sweep the property would be seized it would be demolished a condominium would go up in its place If it didn't burn down first that is I found the room at the end of the hall it was slight and hazy there were some instruments here and there a few crappy sofas KD was there with a guy called Falls and a girl I'd never seen before Falls lived there more or less I had seen him around but hardly knew him Yet like so many others he came on as though we were better acquainted than we were everyone was infected with this strain of imagined familiarity The other girl KD said she'd met her earlier that night at some other place I'll call her Prj She gave the impression of a person trying not to let on she was out of her element I wanted to say this was no one's element or better it was a nonelement a *negative space* We exchanged stories forgotten before they were uttered In this way it followed the normal trajectory and was far less uncomfortable than if we had tried to say meaningful things You do it enough and it becomes rote I had misjudged her I thought

The red sofa was torn and soiled The part where Falls sat was so sunken he was more in it than on it his knees almost touching his chest I thought of him crawling all the way into it at night to slumber amid broken springs bugs condoms candy wrappers KD sat in an adjacent yellow cushioned armchair it was similarly battered and grimy but structurally sound it did not threaten to ingest her In the dusky glow cast by the overhead bulb their eyes were lost in shadow Falls KD and Prj and I thought they might all be dead My elation was tempered by the realization I'd eventually have to explain to someone why I was fine and sentient and they were not I had walked in and found them that way that's all From inside the sinkhole Falls said he'd heard about a party at a motel along the interstate *What* Did we know anyone there Did it matter We were all out of everything so okay yes let's go never mind the bright red flag hoisted at the mention of *motel along the interstate* I rode with Prj in her car Falls with KD in KD's car Swaying up the interstate she said she never did things like this and had a plane to catch in the morning I said it's almost morning Who were these people who caught planes in the morning

After a couple wrong exits we found the motel and pulled into the parking lot KD and Falls were already there No one had perished or gotten hauled to the drunk tank It was a typical downscale chain lodging far from nice but not conspicuously sleazy Falls led the way to the room Inside we found that the party consisted of two people a hulking silent man who sat in a chair in the corner and a girl who had her shirt off and flitted about the room as if doing something important There was a single king-size bed a screen a minifridge a microwave The expected hotel crap art on the walls I'd read somewhere that some bored or pretentious guerilla artists had taken to concealing their own art presumably of a more bracing or radical character behind the mass-produced landscapes and tepid abstracts Subversive messages had also been turning up scrawled inside toilet tank covers or inserted in bibles I thought it not worth the effort to look for them Don't they know the most revolutionary thing you can do is merge with the background kitsch and embrace complicity The shirtless girl introduced herself by listing what she was on Did she have a name It was shuffled amid the names of assorted chemicals some of which were unfamiliar even to me Despite that impressive roster it soon became apparent there was nothing to be had here nothing anyone wanted to share at least Nothing to drink even *And isn't it always that way* KD Prj Falls and me stood around for an uncomfortable minute or two Should we leave Someone was said to be coming who might *have something* and though we were all well acquainted with *that* drama the waiting plot and its bleak dénouement we decided to stay We had already risked death and jail to drive here and there was nothing back at the warehouse either Here if nothing else the tweaked girl provided a facsimile of entertainment So we took seats around the motel room and waited for nothing to happen We had hardly noticed but by then she'd removed her pants as well She still darted around the room on some phantasmal errand Contented I guess that the world was provisionally ordered for now she paused to get up on the bed and invite our opinion of her She leaned back on her elbows *Very voluptuous* KD said with a shitty grin the insinuation was obvious The rest of us responded affirmatively What else would we say The bulky man remained undemonstrative in the corner chair He hadn't said a word the whole time had yielded nothing What relation to the girl what role Protector supplier employer client *Friend* would not do That was not here He was rather I decided an installation piece *Man in Chair* Lazy groping and making out ensued as spontaneous as putrefaction Falls watched from across the room all want and deprivation but he didn't move The day's cumulus of immoderations had caught up with me and things became less distinct There was as always the solemn epiphany as if for the first time that all nights end and it was probably for the best we didn't find what we came for The one whose name was a chemical inventory that would fell a lesser user now had her palms flat against the wall legs spread and Prj who had a plane to catch stood behind and fisted her her slender arm repeating the motion like a robot apparatus designed for this purpose The whole hand would disappear then reemerge fingers extended and pressed together the thumb tucked in With each thrust an agonized cry I expected any minute a bang on the wall or knock at the door It went on for some time I soon stopped paying attention and assumed the same funereal disposition as Falls and *Man in Chair* Even KD was looking down now engrossed in messages We were no longer spectators but inert bodies in the odeum I hardly noticed then when the girl and Prj disappeared into the bathroom Hadn't we dispensed with privacy and discretion what business so indecorous it demanded cloister A minute passed and the former came back out and retrieved a blowtorch from a pile of belongings in the corner She went back in the bathroom and closed the door Falls overcame his paralysis and got up and went in the bathroom as well That left me KD and *Man in Chair* and the stale silent motel-room musk The screen wasn't even on Then a horrible miracle and a smile disfigured the face of the man in the chair I asked KD if she could drive me home but she said she planned to stay a while Should I knock on the bathroom door to remind Prj about her flight I called a driver and went outside to wait

48

It was dinnertime when I got back from seeing the Dr All were more anxious than usual this one perennially displeased with the menu that one all praise but disappointed with the portions what do you mean I can't have ten of those I got mine it doesn't matter what it was and I went and sat in a corner Lycus was always antagonizing *someone* so there were no surprises but this time he'd thrown a plastic spork in someone's face and that person had tried to stab him with it It snapped and the two now grappled on the floor Banal yes but it was enough to get the others worked up and the room tightened like a blood pressure cuff Staff came and *de-escalated* There was less *gore* than in hell yes and ours was a decidedly more pedestrian feast but that was no matter There was no doubt which iteration of eternity had played out

49

One last time I'd stopped by Dehmeck's place the late bus
wouldn't depart for a few hours *One last time* It's true I
had been thinking of endings and irrevocability That lens
alters everything no one looks the same the world is not
what it was Goals become punch lines if you have them
the joke's on you Quiet here not empty but slow Good
On his way to serve someone else Dehmeck looked right
at me and there was nothing You got used to it I had
always melded into scenery but even more so since the
hospital Dehmeck came back around and this time he
recognized me He'd heard some talk he said but wouldn't
elaborate I could imagine but who cares I saw things for
what they were I would catch the late bus it would be the
last time

50

The familiar throb like a vessel might burst mouth full of cotton I had not fucked Tam The truth of that belief was established not immediately but only after a physical investigation and rigorous combing of memory It was early still but the room was already sunny and horrible When I got out of bed everything shifted I almost toppled over There was no rush I had time a few hours at least Enough time to stitch together a provisional self I drank rapidly glasses of water Pills and a long shower and a line and a gulp of liquor Almost there

51

The evening nothing hours Some received visitors The housemates knew I was here I wouldn't have visited any of them either

Zlnka was white last time so it was my turn Twenty options That's far more than most have in life most of the time and I did the ordinary thing what else would I do stick to what you know and pushed the pawn out to e4 He answered by moving his c-file pawn to the fifth rank it too a prosaic thing a common reply There's a name for it they all have names I don't remember now does it even matter knowing that stuff if you don't got the intuition I brought out the kingside knight Zlnka his e pawn D3 to support e4 And with that a pyramidal formation manifested white side it shored up the center and bolstered my defense It looked nice at least that's something else you figure out aesthetics matter too Black knight to c6 his own bid for the center So I slid out another pawn making room to develop the kingside bishop and he did the same I brought out my bishop he did likewise For chrissakes This type of mirrored play unsettles me did he think these were his best moves or was he fucking with me was it a deep strategy or had he no better ideas What could be worse than a mirror If I were smarter I'd set a trap but I'm not smarter I castled and the king was now ensconced in a stronghold comprising three pawns knight bishop and rook Zlnka couldn't copy this because of an obstructing knight so he moved it to g7 presumably intending to castle on the next move In doing so he connected his two knights creating a respectably firm structure I scooted my rook over to further support the e4 pawn and instead of castling he developed another pawn to simultaneously buttress c5 and open a square for his queenside bishop *Center center center* I advanced another pawn to ratchet up the contest for the dark square at d4 He castled and I nudged my pawn to d4 inviting the first exchange of the game Zlnka accepted and then pushed out another pawn proposing further exchange while bidding for more center control Carnage would soon follow This is where the positions thoughtfully established in the opening are altered or sometimes shattered and an upper hand often emerges It was too early to tell however both sides looked artful they were balanced and measured no dim knights on the rim no ragged pawn structures Yet I began to sense this could be the day I trounce Zlnka I'd come close one other time He was off I could tell not just his game but an inching disquiet in his bearing The thought of capitalizing on his compromised state aroused shame but I remembered the point is to win I declined the trade and instead scooted my pawn to e5 Sometimes you know when you've made the right choice even if the precise strategy hasn't coalesced even if the reason isn't clear A spark in the reward system the familiar surge It was the right move Him the queenside bishop me the queenside knight and developmentwise we were roughly matched though I'd insist I still had a leg up with the troublemaking e5 pawn This stretch can seem dull to the casual observer getting all the minor bits into the desired places but the formations established here will be crucial later Zlnka nudged his rook to the semiopen c-file a smart move that tempered my momentum Maybe he wasn't as off as I had thought In response I moved my bishop to f4 lending further support to the e5 pawn and fortifying my center command He took a minute to weigh the next move and then gravely shifted his queenside knight to the edge of the board I blinked He might as well have chucked it across the room When someone makes such a poor move after such deliberation you naturally wonder if it was a brilliant bit of strategy that escaped your notice But no Stronger moves were available moves I had anticipated with concern Instead he violated a basic principle of play and for no good reason Without much thought I positioned my queenside rook to contest his grip on the c-file This was followed by a succession of moves all focused on seizing the queenside He pursued an aggressive attack on my knight and though I brushed off these assaults they were strong moves that helped compensate for his earlier blunder This was more like the player I knew It was time I decided for the queen to intervene I moved the piece out of the imperial box one square no more a multipurpose move that protected some pieces and menaced others with the desired side effect of connecting the rooks And finally Zlnka brought his wayward knight back into the action The board was finely choreographed

now the blocking balanced and connected Beautiful even
The middle was closed Most moves that leapt to mind
could be easily answered The queenside scuffle had settled
for now What next I needed to shift the balance
Something decisive I advanced my g3 pawn to make room
for the e2 knight Zlnka ever fixated on the queenside
extended another pawn down the a-file The smart thing
would've been to dispatch my e2 knight with his bishop
and quash my designs on the kingside right then and there
The next several moves proceeded as if we were pursuing
different games Zlnka aiming to cinch the queenside as I
consolidated my kingside assault He willfully ignored
what was unfolding across the way He did eventually snap
out of it and make a prophylactic move with his knight
In a few more moves all but one of my most powerful
pieces were mobilized kingside Zlnka felt the pressure
now He pursued a series of trades rook for rook bishop
for bishop another rook for rook all rooks off the board
All this did little to hinder my incursion and Zlnka
scrambled to rebuff the offense he had ignored earlier
More trades and captures including a sacrificed white
knight resulting in the black king's defenses being mostly
wiped out Never one to resign Zlnka mounted a desperate
attack with his knight put me in check a couple times all
of which I shrugged off He then took my g6 bishop and
I had to think Most would've done the obvious and
nudged the queen over and taken the knight but it didn't
feel right even though I'd already made one sacrifice
Instead I put him in check with my knight Zlnka's
options were depleted and he knew it

Oppositional That means he's a dick Tonight it was someone called Grgy That Grgy possibly couldn't help it that *bipolar with psychotic features* might have interceded in his choices didn't much occupy my interest The problem is no one can help it and if no one can help it then whatever the reason from where I sit the outcome is the same and Grgy is still a dick even if he *can't help it* It was not unexpected then when he came by and leaned down and brushed the pieces to the floor with a single forearm swipe Maybe this had happened before It was an inherent risk of play in this setting and it kept things casual But I nearly had Zlnka this time and Grgy's head getting slammed into the tile was imagined with ease natural as first love Yes we could have returned the pieces and continued but momentum had withered it was late Zlnka who never had shit to do now had shit to do He also never smiled but now there was an *event* in his face one that redrafted and dislocated it

52

It was night when I got there An outlying neighborhood
it was unfamiliar a few notches above the old
neighborhood rows of sameness all lawns manicured no
cars parked on the street It was dim and quiet I soon
forgot which direction I'd come from there was nothing
to latch on to no way to map or reference The street
names were an inventory of short unmemorable terraces
and courts and spurs Lurching down some Key Avenue
or Good Street I couldn't help but stare inside the houses
when the blinds or curtains were open What did I hope
to see It was all quotidian ritual people planted on the
sofa or at the dinner table Art on the walls that matched
the furniture I passed an alley and caught the smell of
refuse and decided to go that way Behind one lot a riot
of overgrown weeds encroached on the alleyway behind
the next there were well-tended flowerbeds and a
miniature garden I came upon a garage where the
sectional door had been left open It was dark but inside
I could make out lawn equipment a mower shears a rake
There was also a worktable along the left wall I went inside
and grabbed a hammer I saw lying there and quickly

returned to the alley The houses' backsides were nothing like their street façades Over there a set of cellar doors with a layer of bricks on top as if to keep something from getting out An unfinished deck a fire escape ladder attached to a third-story window There were few signs of life except in that one right there a glowing bathroom window and a fuzzy mass moving about behind the steamed-up glass A car blew past down the alley and turned into a carport a few houses ahead It's the ubiquitous things that are invisible to us like the utility poles planted along the alleyway and their unintelligible networks of cable We only notice them when something stops working When I got there the car was still running the driver still inside It was a thing you drove not out of utility but as a signal I stopped just beyond the carport next to a short narrow garage out of sight of car and driver A hollow thumping and knocking came from across the alleyway where some trash bins were lined up along a wooden fence The lid of one of the bins opened and an animal face poked out It climbed out and leapt to an adjacent bin For a static moment the animal looked in my direction and I back at it and then it disappeared over the fence I strode up to the car and smashed out the driver-side window with the hammer Opened the door grabbed the stunned occupant pulled him out I pushed him against the side of the car spots of blood were forming on the left side of his face He was late middle aged well dressed potbellied You bitch you motherfucker He was too shocked to resist when I demanded his wallet I yanked him away from the car shoved him to the ground next to the carport A back-porch light came on and illuminated the carport Was it a sensor or had someone flipped it on

I got in the car backed out into the alley and sped away The whole thing had taken half a minute After some wrong turns I found my way out of the neighborhood drove a while then pulled into an empty lot and searched the car A laptop bag and a phone were sitting on the passenger seat The stereo wasn't worth the effort it would take to rip it out In the trunk there was a suitcase full of clothes and other travel items I jammed as much as would fit into my satchel and walked away

The stuff was spread out on the hotel bedspread My earnings There was abundant cash in the wallet and some credit cards Among the insurance cards the frequent-flyer card the brand-new gym membership ha-ha there was a punch card for a sandwich chain one more and the next meal was free I put it in my pocket The ID said the man was fifty-nine He is an organ donor he requires corrective lenses A name like a character in an office satire There were no photos of spouse children grandchildren paramour in the wallet I examined the clothes some dark slacks a blazer black socks a dress shirt I put the shirt pants and jacket on over the clothes I was wearing All loose but not unwearable and fittingly ridiculous I took the laptop out of the bag powered it up I was tempted to find a workaround for the password ransack the machine to discover whatever sordidness it might contain Perhaps I could blackmail its owner But that was too much bother the planning and execution it gave me a headache No I had already ruined his day

Pawnshops aren't as sleazy as you think And this is too bad Because unloading simple things like that guy's laptop becomes more onerous than it should be I went around to some places You look for storefronts with the veneer of seediness where disreputable folk gather for none-of-your-business backroom commerce Yet with every asshole angling for legitimacy things are not as they appear and the pawnbroking of popular imagination where no one hassles you about stolen stuff is quaint now As expected I got the wary questions and suspicious looks at some places followed by polite refusal I'd all but given up for the day maybe Mrznr could help maybe I'd throw it in the river But then in a suburban strip mall of all places I found some affable brokers who didn't pretend to care where their inventory came from They gave it a cursory inspection then offered more than I thought it was worth

53

Trash blew across the parking lot of the shit motel The interstate was filling with predawn commuters I wondered whether Prj would catch her flight I wondered whether after an anonymous call she would be found unresponsive in the bushes by the motel The driver arrived sooner than expected I was surprised he came at all I settled in for the uncomfortable   and   expensive   half-hour   ride Uncomfortable because I would likely have to talk I didn't like getting around this way but the buses didn't come up here I was out of options

The word recomposed itself and pressed at the gates *More* It even sounds like what it means A persistent nudge toward a good and familiar gravity the way you might crave a snack or long to hold another person When others had closed up shop for the night Haa would usually come through Keeping such hours was his niche his foothold in the market His was a refined understanding of *more* You can peddle crap product as long as the supply is liberal and uninterrupted It mattered to no one that Haa might have had character deficiencies unrelated to his trade That a vendor might do bad things isn't the buyer's concern is it We were halfway to my house when I gave the driver the address I had received from Haa He protested at first he didn't like changing destination midtrip it was against his procedure I thought I might jump out at the next stop were the doors locked would I have to kick out a window But the driver relented when he realized he would earn more fare

People clutching plastic cups milled in the dim front yard in the cold It was an ordinary house in an ordinary neighborhood From the curb I could hear the muted thumping music coming from inside I didn't want to go in but not wanting to do something never stopped me from doing anything The front door was flanked by sidelight windows can't you just smash these things out reach in and unlock the door I thought it would be funny to ring the doorbell Inside I drifted among unknown faces I hesitated to ask if anyone had seen Haa because it would make my intentions known although most were likely doing similar things The DJ was stationed in a corner of the large open living room He manipulated the blinking mixer between the turntables one headphone pressed to his ear his face crunched in concentration a seriousness incommensurate with the task at hand It was dated stuff that had made the dumb journey from mere dreck to respectable schlock I wanted to upturn the table gear records and all Haa was found easily they had formed a semicircle around him and went where he went in formation He held forth on a lot of nothing and none of them listened they had their own nothing to consider I got the thing from Haa with little pain no patter and made

a quick bathroom stop before returning to the living room
Not much is clear after that I remember that one
elongated wall of the room was lined floor to ceiling with
records Two people were standing next to them They'd
pull one out and scrutinize it flip it over exchange some
esoteric babble I saw the house pulsing with flames and
these two hauling crates of them out the door before saving
the dog or cat

That girl is what I took down because I couldn't remember
I was outside waiting for a ride She was there We must've
met inside but that too is lost Pieces of dawn a queasy
glow behind the clouds We got in the car It was someone
she knew I sputtered directions to my place

54

These things I knew I ate and slept better took only what was *prescribed* There was structure and routine How then to stay longer There were the time-honored strategies Toss feces masturbate at breakfast cause some ghastly self-injury But would it work One person gets booted another committed indefinitely Whatever you do there's the risk of *you're not crazy you're an asshole* But that's the same always everywhere isn't it

55

Her father was meeting her later in the morning to help her pack she said She was moving to another state she didn't say which one or why He was driving her there she said That was all I knew I was left to invent the rest I agree it's best to always be reticent but remember that others will fill in the gaps as they please Like this Things had smoldered at both ends for too long the town would end her if she didn't get away too many frayed connections no support prospects for livelihood exhausted it had become stained the place she had loved it was not what it had been in her view the people the streets even were not the same she knew yes though she never said it especially not to herself that removal to a different place would solve nothing she was still her it was not the place that mattered it had worked before she rationalized even though it hadn't she saw this protracted puerility for what it was but this place the new place was a quieter place maybe it would work this time I dumped out what I had left She asked for baking soda and a spoon and water she had her own lighter She was a superior user and I was humbled So I got those things and we did that until it was gone And then the reason we were here the paraphrase of sex that takes place in these circumstances As ever my room was too warm and it was all sweat slick bodies and discomposed hair She said to squeeze her throat I did and as best I could tell it *worked* though I'd always felt in the past I wasn't doing it right how much was too much how invested should you be in the performance of danger and if the thumbs were to shift over the larynx and press decisively what then one housemate saw her come in with me the driver would remember having taken her to my house DNA everywhere and Father would be waiting which meant her absence would be noted in a few hours I'd have to flee immediately change my appearance try to get out of the country and soon hiding out in a dusky motel remorse corroding the ego I would undoubtedly capitulate She gestured for me to release and I did It was over fast after that She facilitated me onto her chest with a certain rote efficiency and there wasn't much talk or lingering afterward She wiped and gathered her clothes from the floor called the same driver who had picked us up earlier And left

56

Refusal seemed stupid you'd get it in the rear anyway
They had to know by now how many times the same
routine a couple drooling meatheads come in hold you
down all your spleen and protest come to nothing I got
to the window and accepted the tiny miracles that made
life better

They brought around the snacks This cherished ritual it
buoyed us intimated the salvation afforded by gray routine
the observance or negligence of which could mean the
difference between going to bed peacefully and self-
enucleation Grace tonight manifested as a plain cheese
sandwich and that was fine we agreed

57

The wind urged her hair into mutiny twirled spires in protest of form and system She was still there at the driveway's end What name some doorstop sound it wouldn't come But then she turned quick pull the quilt back over the window I waited I hadn't put any clothes back on a drop landed on my foot I peeked out again the car was pulling up now she got in and sped off toward Father and packing and a new beginning in a different place I grabbed clothes off the floor to make myself less repellent

58

I put the book away and took out the phone and looked at the screen About two hours had passed since I'd walked down here from the inn The old man was still there across the way in the gazebo It was hotter now The genial late morning had changed mood to an adversarial early afternoon Undeterred by sun and punishment people still thronged the square and the park more now than when I first got here With my free hand I pulled some change out of my pocket

In the city everyone who is not them is an enemy combatant they have no program or purpose except to be that way soldierly and implacable This one was like that the one who got out of the car and went inside at one o'clock I hadn't noticed him before he was younger not soft and slow like the others From here I could make out the number on the cruiser 337

The couple was still there too *he* still on the phone barking instructions *his* face a depthless plane and *hers* a complication of tightened loops and turns The same grackle as before I assumed it was the same returned landing this time on the floor of the gazebo

Two of them two different ones came out of the station now and got in the car I'd seen both before One I had bumped into while leaving the café the other had questioned me the night before outside the library

I stood up The change I had pulled from my pocket dropped to the gazebo floor coins rolled off in different directions *Shit* Startled the grackle flew away I crouched and started retrieving coins with one hand the phone in the other *She* the wife the woman also squatted down to catch a couple that had rolled her way The husband still stood and talked on the phone I was on my knees now and had gathered most of the change I stopped and looked at the phone in my other hand and I tapped the button

59

Dole was asleep or catatonic or expired Hard to tell he was always the same If it weren't for the occasional music of gases pushed through holes or noticing he was in a different position from twelve hours ago his presence wouldn't have registered at all As good as having the room to myself Dole was a multiple attemptee For his troubles all he'd managed was some brain damage and a limp I had botched it once how do you mess up several times Pert the asst burst in clipboard in hand He had the onerous task of checking on everyone every fifteen minutes Some cursory questions how do you feel check off items on the sheet move on He glanced at Dole made a scribble and dashed out These people were alright On a typical day I had more interaction with them than with any other staff and I felt at ease around them Their work was perfunctory no bullshit none of that suffocating concern It wasn't their job I had chatted not uncomfortably with Pert a few times and that never happens He was hurried and overworked like everyone else but his apathy was refreshing

Pert gone Dole unconscious it was a good time to get a shower At least I didn't have to be watched anymore The shower had weird fixtures I'd nearly forgotten what a normal one looked like The warm water trickled more than sprayed the pressure was unsatisfactory and I thought of how the next time I used a regular shower the jutting head would most certainly invite me to affix a ligature to see if it would hold or maybe it would be of the handheld type with its *very convenient* hose I finished up quick so I'd be back by the time Pert the asst returned I switched off all but the recessed amber-colored light near my bed There were no freestanding lamps Because of cords yes but bulbs too lest anyone try to shatter one and ingest the pieces The logic of the death urge I get it but why draw it out make it hurt so much I got comfortable and stared at the ceiling

I opened it to a random page the novel I had found in the *library* which was a single shelf in the common area The idea was that you would take a book and replace it with the one you'd just read Did anyone observe this protocol It was rare that I saw people reading so it's hard to say Usually I couldn't focus long enough to get very far but I thought I'd try in hopes it might ease me toward sopor What I found in the couple pages I slogged through before wanting to blind myself was a fumbling heap of platitudes and stupidity Even I could tell it was careless stuff No this would not do

We are fine we are blank and docile Pert the asst tapped his pen against the clipboard He was relaxed He found us satisfactory He moved on I switched off the light and faded

⌘

I'd been asleep a minute or an hour no more I took it for a dream the sounds radiating from the hall Struggle yelling one especially sharp cry What are called *sleep aids* here you don't understand if you haven't had them I got out of bed and freighted went right to the floor bags of sand stitched into my pajamas But the disturbance persisted I got to the door and groped at the recessed lever In the hall there were three of them two grappling and a third on the floor not moving The third one was Pert the asst his face and head and the floor around his head were a red mess a pen protruded from his eye socket The two who were fighting were Zlnka and a younger person I'd never seen before Zlnka was not young not strong and the other easily wrestled him down and slammed his head into the floor Staff rushing up the hall now but the man on top of Zlnka had already taken Pert's clipboard and pressed one edge into Zlnka's throat pushing with his knee on the other They pulled him off Zlnka and held him facedown on the tile as another injected him Zlnka was still By now several onlookers had gathered in the hall and more staff came along and herded us back to our rooms

JNLXO

Were it not for the hesitation before the fifth rap the sound at the door at exactly seven might have been taken for a cop knock but no the faltered rhythm betrayed something of human vagary He was wide and thick normal height a fat round baby face with a high forehead thick neck swallowed by the collar the head a basketball perched on a charcoal-gray blazer and white button-up The narrow eyes thin scrunched lips short slender nose these slight features all dwarfed by swaths of cheek and forehead barely a chin or jawline to speak of He entered carrying a brown leather satchel He glanced around the hotel room went in the bathroom and shoved aside the shower curtain checked under the sink A coarse region-inflected voice the gruff patois of a rude people asked about the money I gave it to him and he reached into his satchel and pulled out a plastic grocery bag that looked as though it contained a brick Put it somewhere safe and out of sight I looked in the bag a thing akin to a block of soft white cheese wrapped in clear plastic I put it in a drawer and Jnlxo made a face like I'd done something stupid After an uncomfortable moment his expression loosened he unbuttoned his jacket and sat on the bed asked for a drink I grabbed a couple cans from the minifridge and gave him one He popped the tab and took a long drink

Ex-military Jnlxo explained that was how he accessed and got trained on this stuff It was criminal of course for him to have it let alone sell it he'd be put away forever if found out He had a *very secure* lab in his home he said where he manufactured materials Was Jnlxo a halfwit for revealing all this to a stranger It was an easy inference and plausibly correct were it not for his connection to Mrznr Because *connected to Mrznr* carried the understanding that loose lips got burned or wrecked with a hammer or cut off We'll say three-quarter-wit instead Jnlxo crumpled the can in his fist as you do and got another It was then I knew I recognized him The loose familiarity when I opened the door possibly more déjà vu than real memory it had become a fully formed thing But that's not right I should say I recognized his type You see them in bars or psych wards crack houses shelters or the suburbs pathologically disgruntled veterans It's more than trauma it's rage at not felt but actual disposability it manifests as a half-baked retaliatory intent that assumes myriad shapes but almost always accompanies a set of untenable beliefs That's who he was Jnlxo was one of those

For the first few months of the war Jnlxo drove a tank and saw no actual combat He and his crew patrolled areas where the enemy had already been repelled or annihilated by aerial bombardment One evening his commander pulled him aside and told him he was being transferred and he was to gather his things immediately Within minutes Jnlxo was being driven to an airbase It was him the driver and another soldier assigned to watch him No one said anything Jnlxo was put on a plane in the dark Though he wasn't told where he was going he said he believed it was a facility beneath the desert in an adjacent allied nation Once there he received training in the use of high-tech equipment completely unfamiliar to him He assumed he was selected because of his strong technical skills but also because he had demonstrated complaisance and knew how to keep quiet Jnlxo and a handful of other soldiers none of whom he'd ever seen before were taught in great detail how to operate the equipment how to troubleshoot it what to do if it failed but its precise purpose or application was never revealed Was the technology related to advanced weaponry or communications systems or surveillance perhaps The trainees didn't know The soldiers were kept mostly separate and told not to discuss the project among themselves Jnlxo had a private room where he spent hours looking at the walls It was the most privacy he'd had since he'd enlisted and he didn't know what to do with himself Once the training was completed the soldiers were returned to combat each covertly equipped with the new device designed such that it appeared no different from standard soldiers' equipment Alibis were supplied to explain the soldiers' absence and they were ordered with barely veiled threats of retaliation for noncompliance not to disclose anything related to the training or the technology They were directed to activate the device at specific times under specific conditions Jnlxo emphasized that his instructions could've been different from what others were told The operator had to take certain precautions before using the device mainly involving a customized helmet issued to all the trainees It looked the same as a regular helmet but Jnlxo believed it was designed to block the device's effects whatever those might have been   After a few weeks of operating the device as instructed he noticed changes in the other members of his unit They became erratic seized by fits of fear and anxiety even under noncombat conditions Talk of hopelessness and despair became more frequent and one committed suicide about a month after the start of the project Jnlxo explained that while such feelings and behaviors are not uncommon among combat soldiers it couldn't have been coincidental that everyone in his unit except for him was affected simultaneously and with such severity Major operations ended not long after and Jnlxo was swiftly and honorably discharged and sent home with reminders to keep his mouth shut

Jnlxo couldn't put it out of his mind he said the things that happened during his tour of duty so after his discharge and return home he undertook *intensive research* he said and to his surprise there was abundant information *clandestine* yes but still it was *out there* he said and it appeared to explain what had happened to him and his unit The military he learned was secretly testing advanced psyops-related technology on its own troops to determine its efficacy for potential use against enemies Why on their own troops I wondered and Jnlxo tossed down another grand gulp and paused and said the war itself was a ruse orchestrated to cloak a deeper and more far-reaching geopolitical agenda that would otherwise have been condemned by everyone No military action in fact he said is ever transparent in its aims no operation free of latent intent even the reported outcomes are not the actual outcomes All media are servile and complicit all shadow all deception Moreover governments you see he continued had learned from past upheavals from protests and resistance and they had refined their strategies to recast narratives so that antagonists became protagonists fiction and nonfiction indistinguishable words untethered from their meanings The problem he said and then took another drink followed by a protracted exhale is that no one save an elect few understands anything

There was much about the world people like me misapprehended Jnlxo said but I couldn't be faulted since I had no control over the frameworks What I experienced as everyday normalcy was a fabrication engineered to serve the interests of power The worst part he said was that he could see no viable way out Our best hope lay in minor acts of resistance by people like him who had brushed elbows with the truth We talked in this way until there was no more to drink and by the time he left Jnlxo had also shared among other things plans he'd drawn up to overthrow a small country I was invited to come sometime to his *very secure home* where he would show me the blueprints

Accidents are frequent on rest-area entrance and exit ramps
Fatigued truckers lacking more suitable options often park
on them and some unvigilant traveler seeking a snack or
bowel relief or a nice stroll comes along and finds instead
wreckage fire death At least they are delivered from their
discomforts But this was no heavily trafficked interstate
here in the midnowhere all was clear when I got on the
ramp and approached the rest stop There was only a short
line of idling semis in the designated spots and a few cars
I pulled in next to a truck with a mud-splattered ATV
strapped down in the back Why believe in only one extant
human species when the implements of others are
everywhere in evidence I walked to the bathroom It was
empty aside from one person in a stall I went in another
stall and waited for them to finish The stench of another
All those molecules it's sex almost They left I went to a
sink took out the clippers Long strands dropped to the
basin and the floor Did my face as well leaving only a
ridiculous mustache I cleaned up the hair as best I could
then went back to the stall and put on the oversized slacks
dress shirt and blazer There was a tie also but I couldn't

get it right and threw it away Never in my life I put on a large pair of sunglasses and checked the mirror Inside the duffel bag I had packed a smaller shoulder bag I put some essentials in it and left the old clothes and a few other things inside the duffel bag and stuffed it in the trash

The gray sky over the interstate continued to darken This could all end before the first drop falls The car would have to go soon The ID as well It had also been useful but would no longer do There were other Mrznrs The rain began and I fumbled with the controls until the wipers came on Too fast at first but soon I found the right speed The metal arms and black rubber blades swept the surface in harmonious arcs noiseless almost The wipers must have been new the windshield recently washed Things were clear again

ABOUT THE AUTHOR

JOSH WARDRIP's fiction has appeared in *Chicago Quarterly Review*, *Gargoyle*, *New Orleans Review*, and elsewhere. *Forum* is his first book. He lives in Asheville, North Carolina.